One Y...

Four sisters, four s...

When their father dies unexpectedly, the Waverly sisters are set to inherit the beloved outback family estate. The only problem? An arcane stipulation in the will that requires all four of them to be married within a year or they'll lose the farm for good! But with such little time, how on earth will they each find a husband? Well...

Matilda is secretly already married—to a *prince* no less! Now she just needs to track him down...

in *Secretly Married to a Prince*
by Ally Blake

Eve spends a night of distraction with a tattooed stranger, and the consequences are binding!

in *Reluctant Bride's Baby Bombshell*
by Rachael Stewart

Available now!

Ana turns to her best friend for help. But their marriage of convenience is quickly complicated by *in*convenient feelings...

in *Cinderella and the Tycoon Next Door*
by Kandy Shepherd

And Rose makes a deal with the devil: the strip of land his family—and the Waverlys' longtime rivals—has been after for years in exchange for a temporary marriage!

in *Claiming His Billion-Dollar Bride*
by Michelle Douglas

Coming soon!

Dear Reader,

A little over a year ago, at a Romance Writers of Australia conference, Michelle Douglas casually sank into the chair beside mine and uttered the fateful words: "So, I was thinking, we ought to write a series."

From that simple suggestion came ideas, fanciful and impossible, wild and unwieldy. Sisters. Marriages of convenience. Outback and beyond. Next came getting our hooks into Kandy Shepherd and Rachael Stewart, and we were not taking no for an answer.

Cue pages of ideas lovingly filled with setting inspiration and deeply unearthed character descriptions covering the full gamut of the Waverly family, owners of the biggest cattle station in Australia. A family that we fast came to adore. A family about to lose it all.

Most pressingly Matilda, Ana, Eve and Rose—four strong, loving, heart-bruised sisters who would soon have to fight with all they had to save not only their famous home, but also the deep sisterly connection at their cores.

I, for one, will be taking a week off to read our four tales, one after the other. And the tears will flow, both happy and poignant. Tears for our brave sisters and for the truly wonderful time we spent channeling their stories.

Love,

Ally xxx

Secretly Married to a Prince

Ally Blake

Recycling programs
for this product may
not exist in your area.

ISBN-13: 978-1-335-59666-6

Secretly Married to a Prince

Copyright © 2024 by Ally Blake

For questions and comments about the quality of this book, please contact us at CustomerService@Harlequin.com.

TM and ® are trademarks of Harlequin Enterprises ULC.

Harlequin Enterprises ULC
22 Adelaide St. West, 41st Floor
Toronto, Ontario M5H 4E3, Canada
www.Harlequin.com

Printed in U.S.A.

This book is not only dedicated to the wondrous Rachael Stewart, Michelle Douglas and Kandy Shepherd—with whom this book and this series were so lovingly crafted—but to the intricate backstories, and the heartbreakingly deleted scenes, and the deeply curated tales of the Waverly sisters and the Waverly women before them that simply could not make it into the One Year to Wed books if we hoped anyone might be able to physically lift the things.

Praise for
Ally Blake

"I found *Hired by the Mysterious Millionaire* by Ally Blake to be a fascinating read... The story of how they get to their HEA is a page-turner. 'Love conquers all' and does so in a very entertaining way in this book."

—*Harlequin Junkie*

PROLOGUE

Garrison Downs,
June

I<small>T WAS THE</small> first day of winter.

Yet that was not the reason behind the unnatural chill that had settled over the Garrison Downs cattle station. The reading of Holt Waverly's last will and testament was underway.

Matilda Waverly sat curled up on the velvet couch in the centre of her father's large office. The bright cushion she hugged tight to her chest and the fluffy pink jumper she wore over her denim overalls the only bursts of colour amongst all the dark, custom-built wood and masculine brown leather.

She fussed with the ring on her right hand, distracting herself from the strangers milling round the room. Lawyer, accountants, who knew? She wished they'd all sod off, but Rose, Matilda's oldest sister, must have allowed it. For while this day was painfully personal, Garrison Downs was a community, an industry, an economy unto itself, and what happened in this room and how that news was shaped would affect more than just their family.

Rose sat stiff-backed in the guest chair closest to their father's desk. Eyes front, light brown hair pulled back into a ponytail, dust motes floating about her head, as she'd come straight in from checking fences over by Devil's Bend.

Eve, their middle sister, was there in spirit. Or, to be precise, video conferencing from the PR office in which she worked in Central London. Matilda wished she could see *her* face, but since that first minute before proceedings, Eve had been on the screen on the wall behind her.

Hugging the cushion tighter as George Harrington, the family lawyer, droned on about investments, stocks, equipment, trust funds, and the robustness of the station's financial standing, Matilda noted how swamped the older man appeared, sitting behind her father's iconic desk.

Famously featured in most news stories in which her father appeared, the bold antique desk had fit Holt Waverly perfectly. Tough, savvy, immensely respected countrywide, Holt had been a mythical character in modern Australian folklore. An icon.

Dad. *Gone.* Their new reality coming at them in increments. From the accident that had felled him, the outpouring of sentiment from all over the world. The honour—and weight—associated with a state funeral. Only after which had they been able to bury him in the family plot under the shade of a flame tree atop Prospect Hill. Next to their mother, the love of his life.

Matilda blinked to find Harrington had moved on to the gem at the centre of her father's estate. Garrison Downs. One and a half million hectares of red dirt, hills, and vales. Verdant river to the east, ancient craggy outcrops and shadowy canyons to the north. There was the Homestead itself—or "the New House" as those within the family called it—a colossal home built by her parents when Matilda was a toddler, the Old House her father had grown up in, and the Settler's Cottage, a place full of ghosts and snakes and other dangers, which had made it as tempting as it was terrifying when they were kids.

Add a dozen outbuildings, seasonal staff lodgings, machinery, maintenance equipment, feed barns, ghostly gum trees, kookaburras, kangaroos, and sweeping planes of prime cattle grazing land…and it was just home.

Needing something to hug, Matilda clicked her fingers for River, their old lilac border collie— once a working dog, now happier sticking close to home—to come keep her company.

When River didn't instantly appear, Matilda glanced over her shoulder to find the dog sitting in the back corner of the room by a young, dark-haired woman, who was playing with his ear. The woman sat in the chair by the telescope, the chair with the view down the long front driveway. Her mother's favourite chair.

She seemed a little young to be one of the lawyers, and not so slick. She was familiar somehow. Matilda's mouth lifted in a quick smile, her conciliatory nature winning out, even under the circumstances.

The young woman startled as she caught Matilda's eye, before leaning down and saying something to River that had the old dog padding over to Matilda and jumping up onto the couch beside her, panting happily.

Matilda turned to sink her face into River's familiar fur, looking up only when the old lawyer cleared his throat.

"Now to the nitty-gritty," said Harrington, his old voice a mite shaky. "To my daughters, I leave all of the above and all my worldly possessions not listed hereupon, including, but not limited to, the entirety of Garrison Downs."

There, thought Matilda, breathing out. *That's that then. All as it should be.*

Harrington went on, "Let it be known that it is my wish that my eldest daughter, Rose Lavigne Waverly, take full control of the management of Garrison Downs. If that is *her* wish. If not, I bow to her choice."

Rose flinched, then briskly retied her ponytail:

a classic stress move. The passing of the torch no doubt made it all feel absolutely, terribly, irrevocably real. That she was on her own now.

Not on her own, Matilda upbraided, threading her fingers into River's soft fur.

For she'd be there, sprinkling enthusiasm, keeping spirits up. Not because farming was her bliss, but because she knew how it felt to *not* be there when it mattered most. Knew the guilt, the soul-deep bruise it left on a person, and never wanted to feel that way ever again.

"Ah," said the lawyer, glancing over the top of his reading glasses, his gaze settling on some spot over Matilda's left shoulder for a beat, then back to the papers on the desk. "At this point, could we please clear the room of everyone bar family."

A collective wish to stay and not miss a juicy detail pulsed off the walls before the room emptied.

"Now," said Harrington, taking a moment to gift the sisters with a kindly smile. "That was quite the ask, I know. But necessary to cover all the intricacies of your father's will with those who will best help you manage the ongoing running and reputation of the station. There is just one more thing—"

Harrington stopped. Then rubbed his hand across his forehead.

Rose leaned forward; always sensitive to changes

in atmosphere. Only Matilda felt it too, enough that she pulled River a little closer.

"There is a condition placed over the bequest. One that has been attached to the property since its transfer to your family years ago." Harrington took off his glasses and set them atop the papers. "As I'm sure you know, the history of Garrison Downs is complicated, what with your great-great-grandmother having won the land from the Garrison family in a poker game in 1904."

The poker game was legendary in the region. And there was no love lost between the Waverlys and the Garrisons, who still ran another cattle station to the south, though not nearly as big, well-known or prosperous as Garrison Downs.

"Anytime the land has been passed down since, certain conditions had to be met." His hands shook, just a little, as he put on his glasses and read directly from the will. "Any male Waverly heir, currently living, naturally inherits the estate."

"Naturally," Rose murmured.

"But," said Harrington, lifting a finger, "if the situation arises where there is no direct male heir, any and all female daughters, of marrying age, must be wed, within a year of the reading of the will, in order to inherit as a whole."

A sound crackled through Matilda's ears. The past catching up with her? No, Eve was laughing, humourlessly, as if this was somehow no surprise to her.

Some back and forth took place, questions as to what it meant, but Matilda, the history buff of the family, who in her studies had gleefully read about all kinds of mind-boggling hereditary conditions in the lineages of European royal houses, understood all too well.

"The land," Matilda said, her words cutting through the heavy air, "is entailed to sons. If there is no son, the Waverly women *can* inherit—you, Eve, and I—but only if all of us are married."

Protests rose from both of her sisters then, while Matilda's mind stuttered, *married, married, married*, like an old record stuck on a groove.

"It is…arcane," Harrington agreed. "But it has been a part of the lore of this land for several generations. So far as I see it, and so far as your father must have wanted, it stands."

Rose, now up and pacing, shook her head. "How has this never come up before?"

"Sons," said Matilda. "Dad was an only child. Pop only had brothers, though one died of measles and the other drowned, meaning the farm passed straight to him. Waverlys have always been most excellent at having at least one strapping farm-loving son. Until us."

Rose looked to Matilda. Made full eye contact for the first time since the reading had begun. It seemed to shake something loose in her. A flash of real fear, before Rose was back to being Rose. Strong, steady, honourable.

"And what happens if we refuse to…marry?" Rose asked.

As far as Matilda knew, Rose had never had a boyfriend much less a marriage prospect. As for Eve? Who knew what her love life was like—so far away, so busy, so hard to pin down. While Matilda—

Matilda stopped fidgeting with the ring on her right hand and, surreptitiously, sat on the thing.

"If the condition is not met," said Harrington, "the land goes back to the current head of the Garrison family. Clay Garrison."

Rose lost it then. For she had plenty to say about old Clay, and even more about his son, Lincoln.

"Don't waste your time worrying about it, Rose, because that's not going to happen," Eve said, sounding sure. "Not now. Not ever."

Though how any of them could feel sure of anything anymore, Matilda had no clue.

Harrington cleared his throat. "As it stands, unless all four of Holt Waverly's natural daughters are married within twelve months of the reading of this document—"

"Twelve months?" Rose shot back, clearly only *just* having picked up on that bit. "But I can't…

I'm not… I mean *none* of us are even *seeing* anyone right now. Eve? Tilly?"

Matilda shook her head. Slowly. For she wasn't *currently* seeing anyone.

"Wait," said Matilda, stilling a moment, before her socked feet uncurled from beside her to drop to the floor. "You said *four* daughters. There are only three of us."

River jumped to the floor, nudging her knee, whimpering. And the pity in the lawyer's gaze made her sway.

Then, feeling as if someone had taken her by the chin, Matilda turned and looked over her left shoulder to find the dark-haired young woman from earlier, the one who'd been sitting in her mother's favourite chair was still in the room.

"Who *are* you?" Matilda asked, not unkindly.

"Ana," the stranger said, standing and wringing her hands. Her voice was lilting, as if in question.

Eve, now visible to Matilda on the larger-than-life screen, shifted in her seat. "Who are you talking to, Tilly? I can't see."

The chair behind the desk squeaked as Harrington pressed it back and stood. Then he was out from behind the desk, his arm outstretched. "Come forward, girl."

The stranger came forward. A small, hesitant step.

"Anastasia," said Harrington, "this is Matilda

Waverly. That there is Rose. And up on the screen there is Evelyn. Girls, this is Anastasia Horvath."

Ana lifted her hand in a small wave and said, "Hi."

Matilda waved back because...habit. Good breeding. Pathological Pollyanna Syndrome. A deep-seated loathing of all things confrontational. When she glanced back to Rose, it was to find her staring at Ana as if she'd seen a ghost.

"Ana, here," said Harrington, "is your father's daughter. Your half-sister. And therefore, according to your father's will, due an equal share in the estate. And equally beholden to the condition."

The silence that descended over the room in that moment was suffocating. Because... *No.* How?

A half-sister meant... Meant their father had had an *affair*?

The very thought was ridiculous. He'd *adored* their mother. Famously. Their partnership as legendary as the land they ran.

Then there was the way they had met—a whirlwind, love at first sight, holiday romance between big, gruff, cattle baron Holt and brilliant, elegant, titled socialite Rosamund, after which he swept her home and they'd lived happily ever after. Until Rosamund's sudden death several years before.

That story was foundational. The keystone to their family.

And he'd had an *affair*?

"Impossible," Matilda whispered, only realising she'd said it out loud when Ana flinched.

While her heart shook, rejecting the very thought, Matilda looked harder. Ana appeared younger than her by a smidge. Her hair was dark and straight, compared to the shades of light brown to blond shared by Rose, Eve, and Matilda. But her eyes—that vibrant piercing blue—they were their father's eyes.

Matilda's hand, the one that had waved, dropped to her side, feeling as heavy as lead.

"Rose, Eve, and Matilda, you still have the trusts your mother left for you," said Harrington, dropping to sit on the arm of Matilda's couch.

Her eyes moved to him, the easier target. He looked tired. As if the past few weeks, leading up to this day, this bombshell, must have been hard on him too.

"They exist outside of the scope of the conditions. So don't fret on that. But the land itself, the Garrison Downs station and all of its holdings, will belong to the Garrison family unless you, Rose, Evelyn, Matilda, *and* Anastasia, are all married within the next twelve months."

This was real. *Really* real. Meaning they had to get on the same page, and fast.

Which was where Matilda usually came into her own. As the youngest, it had fallen to her to find some creative way to lighten the mood. But all she could think was that she had information that might bring a modicum of relief.

"Rose?"

"Hang on. Evie, did you *know*? Is this why—"

"I have to go," said Eve, looking as pale as the white walls surrounding her. Before the TV turned to black.

"Ah, Rose—"

Rose threw out her arms and stormed toward the office door. "I can't—I don't have time for this. I have a station to run." At the door she stopped, turned, pointed at Ana and barked, "Stay!" And then she was gone.

Matilda knew Rose didn't mean to sound so autocratic, that she was used to having to deal with brash young station hands testing her authority on the daily, but the situation meant everyone was tense.

Including Matilda, who swallowed the words she'd been readying to spill, a secret she herself had been keeping for several years, with a discomfiting level of relief.

From somewhere inside the house they all heard Rose holler, "Lindy! Can you see that the yellow guest suite is made up for Anastasia please. She'll be staying with us for a bit."

She would? Matilda thought. Then, *Yes, she would.*

For Anastasia was clearly as crushed by the

whole situation as the rest of them. And she was here, on her own.

This was their father's fault. Every last drop.

He'd *left* them, not only when Rose, Eve, and she were so young, to have an affair with some other woman, but he'd left them again, with this 'condition' hanging over them like an anvil about to drop on their heads.

He'd left them with nowhere to put their shock, their anger, their hurt. No one to ask why.

As rage, and fear, and panic rose inside of her, Matilda too would have loved to have flicked a switch and shut it off. Or walked out of that now claustrophobic damn room, and outside, where she might scream at the wide blue winter sky.

But the clock had already started ticking.

One year.

One year to wed or lose the land that had been their lifeblood, their safe space, their connector since birth.

Rose, for whom Garrison Downs was the love of her life.

Eve, who was not exactly known for toeing the family line.

And Ana...

From the corner of her eye, Matilda glanced at the girl, only to see that she was shaking like a leaf, her bright blue eyes glassy, as Harrington gently tried to talk her out of leaving.

Dad, Matilda thought, a ball of fury clenching

in her belly. *How could you? Why would you? Did Mum know? Oh, poor Mum. How dare you do that to her? How dare you do this to us?*

Then again, she thought, her thumb once again playing with the ring on her right hand, when it came to family secrets, who was she to protest?

Matilda closed her eyes. Trying to find a kernel of anything in her life that she could trust anymore.

Rose. Eve. *That* she could trust. Her sisters.

Matilda turned to face Ana. For she was in this now too.

Fortifying herself with a big breath, Matilda offered up a smile. Gave her a nod. Letting her know it would all be okay.

Matilda would make sure of it.

And the clock was ticking.

CHAPTER ONE

Chaleur,
one month later...

MATILDA WAVED TO the taxi driver.

"Bonne chance!" he called, waving back happily as he drove away. His grin was no doubt due to the generous tip she'd added on top of the fee for the trip from Nice Côte d'Azur Airport to Côte de Lapis, a coastal town in the picturesque principality of Chaleur.

Or it could be the fact she was no longer in the car, talking his ear off.

"What's in Côte de Lapis?" he had asked as he'd angled his way out of the airport queue. "We have lovely beaches here in France."

"I'm not after a beach," Matilda had said. "I'm looking for a man."

"We have those in France too," said the driver, eyebrows waggling at her in the rearview mirror.

"A specific man," she'd said, smiling. Then frowning. Because it wasn't a laughing matter at all. In fact, in the space of a couple of months, life for the Waverly sisters had become a big old mess.

Rose was still deeply mourning their dad—his physical loss *and* the loss of the man they'd thought him to be—while also frantically trying to fill his shoes.

Eve, still resolutely sticking it out in London, was proving even more bull-headed than usual—flat out denying the condition of bequeathment in their father's will was valid. While acting as if Ana didn't exist at all.

As for Ana, in the short time they'd had together before she'd gone home to her family, it had been clear how overwhelmed she was feeling. Navigating a life with sisters she'd never known, all of whom looked at her and saw their father's betrayal, was hard enough without the pressure of the will.

Then, there was Harrington, the lawyer, still insisting the will was as their father must have wanted.

Add the need to keep the will condition under wraps, so that the vultures didn't start circling, and to keep Ana's existence private for as long as possible, and it was near impossible to call on outside help with any assurance it wouldn't blow up in their faces.

Meaning, as far as Matilda saw it, it was up to her to figure out a plan.

"Ahh," the taxi driver had said, "is this a dating

app scenario? Or you are a woman scorned?" He sounded intrigued more than accusatory.

"No! No, nothing like that. It's a man I…I *knew* some time ago. A man I very much need to track down again."

Though after two solid weeks of searching, she was fast losing hope of finding Henry at all.

Henry. Her not so little secret that had finally come home to roost.

She'd been nineteen when they'd met, having skipped off overseas midterm in the final year of her history degree in search of an infamous, missing, handwritten love letter her favourite professor had been wanting to authenticate for years. Keen to follow in his footsteps and become a renowned graphologist and authenticator of celebrated letters herself, she'd flown to Vienna with the intention of making his dream come true.

But the truth of it was she'd been looking for an excuse to do something wild and wondrous for years, having been told tale after tale of exotic adventure by her well-travelled mother in lieu of bedtime stories since she was a little girl.

What she hadn't counted on was meeting a boy. A boy named Henry.

When she'd caught his eye across that crowded bar in Vienna, *phew*, that had been a moment. The way his thick dark hair swept across his forehead, somehow immaculate and unkempt all at once. The pale hazel of his bedroom eyes. The most perfectly carved lips. Pale skin that flushed pink in the cold. Then there were squiggly horizontal lines furrowed permanently into his brow, making him appear deeply thoughtful, über-masculine, and tragically Byronic all at once.

Like lines of verse, Matilda used to think.

The kind he was always reading her from that beaten up, blue, leather-bound book of letters and poetry she had bought him from a second-hand bookstore in Paris.

All of it had been made even more enticing by the fact he was one of a crew of bright young things who knew nothing about one another bar their names.

That had been the deal. Something she'd discovered when Andre, Henry's cousin, had swooped on her at the bar in Vienna after having seen the way she and Henry had been swooning over one another, laying out "The Rules".

They were a wandering band of merry travellers having what he called a Summer of Freedom.

Their intent: suck the marrow out of life before responsibility and consequence sucked the life out of them.

Their terms: names only, no talk of home or family. No selfies or group photos.

Anyone found to breach the rules was out. Cut off. Left behind.

From the outside it had had all the hallmarks of a cult, but she'd known their ilk in boarding school. Bored, cloistered rich kids desperate to break free.

Besides, she'd helped her dad break horses and birth calves, told off grizzled stockmen for swearing in front of her gran. She could take any one of them without breaking a sweat.

Yes, she probably ought to have thought through the logistics, and the why, but it had been so thrilling, and a million miles from where she'd grown up. She had, with intent, put herself in adventure's path and adventure had *found* her. And the lure of anonymity, of adventure, had been too strong.

As had the lure of Henry. Enough that one night, off the coast of Gibraltar, by the power vested in the yacht 'captain' who'd sailed them there, she had vowed to love him through all her forevers.

A whirlwind wedding, a fairy-tale romance— it had mirrored the way her parents had met so beautifully it had felt meant to be.

Only later that same week, as if her karma had swung so far past the edges of exhilaration her life had overcorrected, she'd learned that her mother was dying.

By the time she'd made it home, it had been too late. The household in disarray, her father crushed, Rose a shadow of herself, there had been no time to tell them her 'good news'. It had felt cruel to have been that happy at the same time her mother had been so unwell.

There was the fact that Henry hadn't followed, hadn't even been in touch, even after she'd broken the rules and left a note telling him how. With no way to contact him, no information bar his name, she'd never seen him again.

After such severe romantic whiplash, she'd hunkered in, put her head down, burned through her studies, put all her love into the family she had left, and lived as if none of it had been real.

Until George damn Harrington had read out the conditions of her father's damn will.

The taxi driver had sighed, a gloriously Gallic sound. "I know that look in your eyes all too well. This man, he is the one that got away."

"Mmm…" she'd said, noncommittally, while shifting uncomfortably on the car seat. "The thing is, I've been looking for a couple of weeks now. Hitting places we'd been together. But staff have moved on, places have closed down. The trail is getting cooler and I'm running out of options."

"Can you not call him? Knock on his door?"

"All I have is his name. It was a thing."

The driver had cocked his head, as if he had misjudged and ought not to be encouraging her on what seemed a fool's mission. But whatever he saw in her face, her ragged last vestiges of hope, had him shaking his head in a fatherly manner and saying, "Have you tried stalking him? On the…*comment dit-on*? On the socials?"

She had. With no luck.

"Mmm," the driver had said, "let me think on it."

Leaving Matilda to slump back in her seat and worry that, while thinking his name still brought on warm swoopy feelings inside her, echoes of the way he'd made her feel all those years before, he might not remember her at all.

What if he was some weirdo who collected wives then let them go with nary a word? What if he wasn't a weirdo, but had changed? Irrevocably? What if he wasn't exactly as she remembered him? What if he *was*?

What if he was *with* someone? What if he had married again, and she was about to open a massive can of worms?

What if she never found him at all? Or never found proof that they'd said *I do*? Did that mean the condition would be impossible to fulfil right from the start, and it was all her fault?

"What is his name?" the driver had piped up. "This man of yours?"

"Henry," she'd said, a hopeful lilt at the edge of the word. "Henry Gallo."

The driver had looked front, his expression thoughtful. Then he said, "I thought it rang a bell, but I have nothing."

Now, standing on the beach path, one hand waving as the taxi driver edged his way through the lethargic traffic, the other resting on the handle of her small suitcase, Matilda took a deep affirming breath and checked out Côte de Lapis.

Bougainvillea cascaded down the pastel-stuccoed facades of centuries-old buildings tucked up together on the other side of the curving coastal road. Tables and chairs, and pots of brightly coloured flowers took up every spare inch of footpath, with café after café taking advantage of the view of striped umbrellas lining the craggy beach behind her, and beyond that the glinting Mediterranean.

It was exquisite. And dripping with history. But no matter the urge to soak herself in it till her fingertips turned pruney, she wasn't there to sightsee.

She was there to find Henry.

To convince him to stay married to her for one more year, on paper at least, in order to fulfil the provisions of her father's will, after which they could shake hands and move on with their lives.

And then—if they couldn't find some other way out—her sisters might magically meet wonderful men to love and marry and it would all work out. It had to. The alternative was unthinkable.

As if on cue, her phone rang.

"Rose!" she answered. "Everything okay?"

"Just checking in," said Rose, her voice overloud as if she was outside. "Still in Paris?"

"Nope. I just arrived in Chaleur."

"Oh." Then, "And where is that exactly?"

"Tiny principality in a crook of the south of France." Matilda laughed. "Let me guess… If it doesn't import Waverly beef, it might as well not exist?"

"True that."

"Now, Tilly, remember," said Rose, her tone dropping into serious big sister mode, "while you will undoubtedly become best friends with every person you happen upon, use discretion. If news gets out—about the will, or Ana—"

"So the T-shirt I had made, the one that says Marry Me or I Lose the Farm, you want me to take it off?"

"I'd appreciate it," Rose deadpanned. Then, "Now go poke an old building, look at mouldy statues, sniff a tulip. Whatever people do over there."

"All those things," Matilda assured her. "Now you remember, Boss, since I'm not there to remind you every minute of every day, you could run that place with one hand tied behind your back, and you'd still do so with grace and aplomb."

A pause. "I'm currently knee-deep in bore water and smell like cow dung."

"And yet, I bet," said Matilda, "glorious with it."

With that, the sisters hung up.

Reinvigorated in her quest, Matilda tipped up onto her toes and peered over the top of the traf-

fic, checking the faded names on the café aw-
nings. Searching for one name in particular.

Though they'd not visited Chaleur, Andre,
Henry's cousin, had mentioned a café in Côte
de Lapis more than once. Either his family owned
it, or they had the best coffee in Europe. She
couldn't quite remember, but there was some connection.

There. Beneath the yellow and white awning,
café tables, small dogs loosely tied up to wrought
iron chair legs, friends meeting, cheeks bussing,
a cacophony of style and colour and life, just as
Andre had described it. Café du Couronne.

Her stomach swooped again, for it was a real
place, and still standing. Or maybe that was hunger. Now she thought about it, she was starving.

She looked both ways, found a path through
the slow-moving cars ignoring the lane mark-
ings entirely, and made her way to the other side
of the road.

Where she would find a waiter, say, "Hey! I'm
looking for an old friend. Henry Gallo? Wondering if you might know him."

But first, coffee.

Henri rested his elbow on the rim of the convertible car window and listened with half an ear as
the news journalist on the car radio showed mild
hope over the improved state of the economy,

then moved on to the lack of royal family attendance at the Summer Festival celebrations.

When there was no hint of a clandestine meeting between the Sovereign Prince of Chaleur and a handpicked gathering of sympathetic members of both sides of parliament, the subject of which would have generations of royal ancestors turning in their graves, Henri switched the radio to silent.

His gaze skimmed over the traffic ahead. Cars had slowed to a crawl or a stop both ways, as drivers and passengers alike gawked at the view.

Boris and Lars, the security detail in the car behind, would not be impressed with the crowd or the delay. But impressing them was not on his top ten list of things he had to do that day.

Finding himself with a rare moment of nothing to do, Henri tipped back his head and breathed in the sea air. Côte de Lapis in summertime with its quaintly colourful architecture, plethora of shops and cafés, creamy sands dotted with striped umbrellas, and water the colour of sapphires, was a local jewel.

In fact… Henri sat taller, looking over the top of the cars to the string of cafés across the road.

And there, beneath the yellow and white awning, was Andre's old place. Café du Couronne. The Crown Café. Not the most subtle man on the planet, his cousin. Why he'd given the place up, Henri could not remember.

Though it was around *that* summer. The Summer of Freedom, as Andre had labelled it, once again lacking finesse. It had been a hell of a time, either way. The only time in Henri's life he'd been able to relax, dispute, go anywhere, make questionable choices, make love, and just disappear, all without needing to consider anyone but himself.

It was the summer that everything changed.

The car beside his moved a few inches, giving him a direct view to the café. To a table where a woman sat, alone.

Messy blond waves tumbled down her straight back, her shoes were tipped up onto their toes, and her finger trailed up and down the handle of her coffee glass.

And Henri was hit with a wave of déjà vu, of *longing*, so strong it slammed him back in his seat.

Hands gripping the steering wheel, tight enough the leather groaned, he forced himself to face front. For it wasn't *her*. It couldn't be. It was his mind playing tricks, having harked back to 'that summer'.

And yet… He turned and squinted the woman's way, as if it might encourage her to turn. Just a little. Just enough so that he could be sure.

A waiter stopped by the woman's table, leaning a hip against it as if settling in. He tipped his chin, asked her a question, then laughed, head tipping back as he guffawed. Which did nothing to assuage Henri. For that had been *her* way. Pure energy, like summer sunshine, collecting hearts indiscriminately.

And then the woman turned, ever so slightly, tucking her hair behind one ear in a move that made Henri's chest ache. The feeling was akin to stepping into an ice bath, for it had been some time since he'd allowed himself to feel much of anything at all.

Look over, he begged silently. *Look this way.*

A gust of warm wind carrying the scent of brine from the Mediterranean washed past him before lifting leaves from the road, shaking the yellow and white awning.

Then the woman stilled. And slowly, as if time was playing games with him, she began to turn his way.

A car behind him hit its horn, and Henri, caught halfway between the past and this moment, took his foot off the brake, only to hit the back of the car in front. A tap. The slightest nudge. But enough for the driver's arm to fly out the window, a string of curse words in vibrant French following, before the driver's door whipped open and he got out of his car.

Henri switched off the engine and dropped his head. Then, as he alighted from the car, Boris was there, flanking him, while Lars moved quickly to placate the other driver, who was now gesticulating as if it was the end of the world.

Yes, he was wearing sunglasses. Yes, to the untrained eye, he was just another man in a suit. And he lived in such a way that he was not nearly as recognisable as his father and his uncle before him. Yet when the other driver saw Henri, he paled.

He then gesticulated to the gods in apology, before he began bowing and apologising profusely. Creating enough of a scene to draw the attention of those in cars nearby.

"Sir," Boris intoned, as he too could feel the shift in the atmosphere.

"Yes, I'm aware." Henri made to slip back behind the wheel only to find people were now holding up their phones. Whispers spinning out into the crowd. Tourists, walking the beach path with their zinc noses and Turkish towels, slowed and pointed.

Across the road, café chairs squeaked, and patrons turned, shielding their eyes to the glint off the water to see what was going on. Including, Henri noted, the blonde in blue.

Then her eyes found his.

Time seemed to stop, then swell and contract, as the world around Henri blurred, leaving only those big blue eyes and that lovely, achingly familiar face.

Matilda, he thought, as she pressed to standing

so quickly her chair rocked. Then lifting to her toes, she raised her hand in a frantic wave.

What could Henri do but lift a hand and wave back.

Which only led to a rousing cheer from the gathering crowd, as if that one small move had given them all permission to engage.

"Henri! Henri, over here!"

"Where 'ave you *been*?"

"*Je t'adore*, Henri!"

"Henri! Marry *me*!"

For generations the more extended sections of family had lived openly, gone to local schools, worked regular jobs, moving in society in such a way that they were treated with respect but not shock and awe.

Only, since taking on his current role, Henri had not. Nor had he leaned into the more ceremonial parts of the job. Choosing, instead, to spend his time doing work that made a real difference.

In that moment his chickens came home to roost.

"Boris," said Henri.

The large man moved in. "Sir. We can get you out of here. Just say the word."

"Not quite yet," said Henri, lifting the edges of his mouth and waving at the crowd, who all cheered as one. "I need you to do something for me. The blonde woman on her own in the Café du Couronne. Bright blue eyes. Australian accent. If she is amenable, can you find a way to bring her to me?"

"Sir?" Boris blinked, nonplussed, then glanced across the way. For Henri had never asked Boris to bring him a girl before.

"Ce n'est pas comme ça," Henri insisted. "Her name is Matilda. She is an…old friend. Of Andre's."

Which was true. Just not the whole truth, which sat uneasily on Henri's shoulders. Was this how it had started for his uncle? His father? A small secret here, a bigger lie there? In for a penny, in for a pound?

But considering the subject of the meeting he had *just* left, the last thing he needed was the slightest whiff of scandal. And this moment had all the ingredients of a perfect storm.

"Boris," he said, angling his head toward the other side of the road.

"Yes, sir." Boris whistled to catch Lars's attention, twirled his hand in some bodyguard signal that meant *Finish up with the other driver and cover Henri as I have to go see about a girl.*

Once Lars was at his side, his general air of *I will bite off your head if you come too close* keeping the crowd at bay, Henri caught the eye of a woman nearby. Then an older man. Then another.

Not a crowd. People. *His people.* Their interest his interests, their concerns his concern. Everything he did, and was putting in place, was for them.

Despite his lack of match fitness in such public situations, and Lars's panicked gaze, Henri reached out to shake a few hands and answered any questions of those brave enough to ask. Most of which seemed to hinge on asking how *he* was.

"Sir?"

Henri turned to find Boris had returned. And with him…

Matilda, he thought, his throat constricting. For the last time he had seen her, she had been fast asleep, her lashes dark against her cheeks, while he'd felt full from the promise of all the days that lay ahead.

It had become habit for him to let her sleep, as the nights had been spent doing anything but. He'd kissed her forehead, taken the speedboat to the mainland so as to get in a run, grab coffee and supplies. When he'd returned, all that remained of her was an indent on her pillow, her scent on the sheets, and a note.

"Henry?" she said, snapping him from his fugue. And thank goodness. For he was surrounded by a hundred of his subjects, many now bearing mobile phones.

"Matilda," he said, the rough catch in his voice unavoidable.

Then she smiled, and laughed, her eyes bright, as if this was all so lovely and unexpected, and years' worth of attrition didn't loom between them like an unassailable gulf.

Then she tilted her head toward Boris. "Either Andre has had quite the makeover or this is a new, rather assertive, friend you've made."

"That would be Boris," said Henri.

"Hey, Boris," she said, hitching the strap of a bag, and readjusting her grip on a suitcase, a flutter of blue ribbons drooping from the handle. "Nice to meet you."

Henri shot Boris a look, after which the big guy turned away to join Lars in keeping the crowd at bay.

And when Henri's gaze once again met Matilda's, it was her giving him a lazy once-over. As if she too was swimming against a tide of memories. And he felt a flicker inside of him—a rebound of the instant spark that had drawn them together all those years ago.

When someone called his name, and others took up the cry, Matilda looked up and around, understandably bemused to find herself in the middle of the street surrounded by beeping cars and strangers pointing phones their way.

Remembering himself, Henri drew on the diplomatic skills drummed into him from birth, and asked, "Do you have somewhere to be?"

"No, no plans."

"Might I suggest somewhere not quite so

crowded?" He motioned to the gridlock. "So that we might catch up?"

"Yes!" she said, nodding vigorously. "That would be great."

Henri turned to Boris, who had not moved far, and beneath his breath said, "Time to go."

Boris nodded. Another whistle, and he and Lars had the crowd moving back, cars shifting, making space.

Henri looked to her bags. "Is there anything else we need to collect. A car perhaps?"

"It's just me. I came straight from the airport to head to that café over the road, as Andre had mentioned it was a favourite. I was literally just about to ask a waiter if he knew you and there you were—as if I'd conjured you out of thin air."

She smiled again, that bright wide sunshiny smile that had, once upon a time, dazzled him. Meaning it took a moment for her words to sink in.

She was here looking for him?

Henri caught Lars's eye, motioning to Matilda's bags. Time to go.

Lars swept in, took Matilda's luggage, and hoisted it into the back seat of the convertible. Then, not wishing to appear completely inept, Henri moved around the car to open the passenger side door.

He watched Matilda move with as cool a level of disinterest as he could manage—that bounce in her step, the swish of her hair, the way her eyes were constantly on the move, cataloguing every sight, every sound, every detail, as if the world had been drawn for her benefit. Then he made the mistake of breathing in as she swept past him. Apple-scented shampoo and warm feminine skin.

A quick glance out to sea, then up into the sky—calling on any gods who might be listening, asking them to gift him forbearance—he jogged back to the driver's side and leaped into the seat and turned the key.

As ever, the grunt of the engine spurting to life called to something inside of him—for it was the sound of freedom. Something he'd had very little of in his life.

Having been let off the leash, Boris and Lars worked their magic and miraculously cleared a path. Encouraging cars to angle away, others to nudge up onto the beach path, so that their prince could pass.

CHAPTER TWO

MATILDA TWIRLED HER hair into a low bun, stray strands whipping across her face as Henry drove them up, up, up into the craggy seaside cliff face looking down over Côte de Lapis.

The view was breathtaking. The deep azure of the water, the sun shining softly on the tightly packed dwellings dotting the cliffside. It was so wildly different from the red dirt and wide-open vistas back home, she barely let herself blink lest she miss a single thing.

The engine purred as Henry took the car down a gear, hugging a sharp curve in the cliff and yanking her back into the sharper reality.

Henry. She was in a car with *Henry*.

The suit and tie were new, as was the cool in his eyes. This Henry was stiff-backed as opposed to laid-back. But the bolt of awareness that had corkscrewed through her the moment their eyes had met was exactly the same.

Not that that would be a problem. For not only did the truth of her parents' fractured marriage have a tight grip on her heart, the stakes were just too high. There was also the fact that Henry hadn't exactly seemed *delighted* to see her.

Though he had suggested finding some place "not quite so busy" so that they might "catch up," which had to be a positive, right?

Where had all those people come from? Some sort of parade, or protest? It had come out of nowhere.

But in the end, all that mattered was that she'd found him. She'd found *Henry*.

Matilda turned to face him, slowly, aiming for subtle as she made to check him out.

He rested his elbow on the windowsill, the hand on the wheel loose and relaxed. He'd loved driving back then, a little fast but fully in control. Now his face told a different story. The furrows in his brow seemed deeper. Behind his sunglasses his eyes flickered as if he was chasing a flurry of troubling thoughts. Her showing up most likely one of them.

His hair was still matinee-idol dark, though he'd tempered the natural tousled wave. She used to play with it, curling her fingers against the back of his neck when he drove. The memory of him relaxing into her touch, one hand on the wheel, the other moving to her knee, his thumb stroking her thigh, was so strong she had to curl her fingernails into her palms.

She must have made a sound—probably a lusty

sigh—as he turned to face her, his eyes hidden behind his sunglasses, before his gaze went back to the sharply curving road.

The moment was brief, and yet her insides twisted, roiling with echoes of how they had been. Followed by the thud of how easily it had all come undone.

Thankfully the air cooled as they left the cliff face and drove up into the hills, past beautiful old homes with mossy stone walls, plots of pretty farmland, before cutting through ancient forests of dark green pines casting cool shadows over the curving road.

Matilda sat up, the seat belt cutting into her shoulder as a castle came into view. Sandstone warmed by the soft Chaleurian sun, medieval windows, fairy-tale turrets and spires, built into a rocky outcrop in the foothills of the distant mountains.

"What is that place?" she said, her voice catching on the wind.

Henry's finger swiped across his mouth before it moved back to the wheel. "Le Château de Chaleur."

"Le Château de Chaleur," she repeated. How many generations of letter writers might have scribbled their fears, their regrets, their hopes, love won and lost onto the page in such a place? "Is it abandoned?"

"It is not," Henry confirmed. "It is home to the royal family of Chaleur."

"How charming."

Matilda knew little about Chaleur. Small in area and population, it was overshadowed by its bigger, flashier neighbours. Though, so far, it was exactly the kind of place her mother would have loved; secluded, unexpected, and breathlessly beautiful.

Soon the trees gave way to a long tall wall, built of the same sandstone as the castle they'd seen in the distance. Wild red rosebushes lined its length while ivy gripped its heights, giving the place serious *Beauty and the Beast* vibes. Which were only heightened when the car slowed, turned, and pulled up to a set of gates; two stories high, made of thick wrought iron twisted into sharp thorny shapes.

Then the gates began to open, slowly, groaning like some ancient slumberous giant, and Henry's convertible hugged the long, neat, curving gravel drive until they pulled up beneath the portico of le Château de Chaleur.

Matilda's hair settled about her shoulders as the car came to a stop. The wind now gone, her ears rang with the silence.

She screamed, then swore rather loudly, as something opened her door, only to find Henry's friend Boris standing there. Not her finest moment.

She uncurled herself from the car to find the

other big guy, the one who'd swiped her luggage, standing by another car. A hulking great black beast with dark windows.

"Do you *work* for Henry?" she asked, when what she really meant was *Why are you following us and what am I missing?*

"Hen-ri?" Boris asked, an eyebrow scooting north, his pronunciation more *On-ree* than regular old Henry.

Though Matilda was soon distracted by the sight of the man himself prowling around the front of the car. All slow purposeful strides, furrowed brow, cool gaze, and sharp angles.

The Henry she'd known had been a romantic, a seeker, this *On-ree* had an edge of otherness, of disconnection that sent a chill down her spine.

Which was probably a good thing. A clear separation of then and now.

Hand on the open car door, she said, "It was lovely of you to stop here—you know I love a castle—but I'd love to have that catch-up you mentioned. I can find my way back here, another time."

Suddenly a team of what could only be servants spilled from the front doors of the castle, speaking fast French, then hauling Matilda's bag and luggage away.

"Wait! What? Sorry, can you bring that back, *s'il vous plaît*?"

"Why don't you come inside?"

She glanced up to find Henri beside her. His hand on the car door beside hers. His nearness made her sway. *Actually sway.* Her hand jerked, brushing his, sparks shooting up her arm. She tugged her hand free. As did he, his thumb running down his palm as if her touch had burned.

"Freshen up, after your flight. Then we can talk," he said, his voice lower, more intimate. He lifted an arm, ushering her toward the front door.

Come in, he said. Not *go in.*

"Who *are* you?" she asked.

His gaze remained cool. As it had in the middle of the street, surrounded by the crowd, but not a part of it.

But if he thought he could out-stubborn a Waverly, he was about to learn a hard lesson. Matilda crossed her arms, her eyebrows lifting in question.

"Let's assume the statute of limitations on Andre's Privacy Pact has long since passed." She held out her hand, deep inside Henry's personal space, and out of the corner of her eye saw Boris take a step their way.

"Hi," she said, "I'm Matilda Waverly. I was born and bred in Garrison Downs, a cattle station in South Australia. I am an authenticator of old letters, by trade. I have two—" *Dammit.* "Three sisters. An aversion to any food that wobbles. What else? My favourite colour is blue—"

"Matilda," Henry said, his voice chastising but

also, somehow, indulgent. As if he was enjoying her riposte, despite himself.

"Who. Are. You?"

She watched as a dozen thoughts tangled behind those pale hazel eyes, before he said, "I am Prince Henri Gaultier Raphael-Rossetti."

He pronounced his name *On-ree*.

A burr of pain settled behind her ribs. For while she'd known next to nothing about him, she'd thought at least he'd given her his true name.

Then her brain stuttered and she backtracked a smidge. "I'm sorry, did you say *Prince*?"

He nodded. Though it was more of a gentle bow. Elegant, practiced, princely.

Matilda blinked. "Since *when*?"

"Since birth," he said, a flicker at the edge of his mouth that might have been a smile. Or a grimace. "Though I have been Sovereign Prince of Chaleur for the past two years."

Matilda looked at the ancient sandstone structure, the burly bouncers hovering nearby, Henri's gorgeous car, and the beast parked in behind it. She remembered the crowd in the street, surrounding him, calling his name.

Then she looked back at *him*. The way he held himself, the way he dressed, the way he spoke. How educated and hungry for knowledge he had been back then. That *je ne sais quoi* that had drawn her in from the very first moment.

"Are you freaking kidding me?" she asked.

"I am not. Freaking or otherwise." Again with the flicker at the corner of his mouth. This time it came with a slight thawing in his gaze.

The requirement of anonymity, the money, the access, the way they had breezed through Europe with absolute entitlement. It all made sense now. It hadn't been a weird hazing thing, or bored rich kid thing. It had been about protecting Henry.

A *prince*.

A prince that she had fallen for. Had married. Which made her...

No. Nope. Nopetty no. There was no point getting ahead of herself. Not until she had legal paperwork before her own eyes. Legal enough to satisfy George Damn Harrington.

As to the rest? Part of her wanted to kick him, right in the shins, for keeping such a thing from her. Then again, she had vowed to love him for a lifetime, before bolting to the other side of the world. Maybe they were even.

Finding it within herself to choose amity, for she needed him onside, she said, "Well, it's nice to finally meet you, *On-ree*." Then, "But if you think I'm going to curtsy, you have another think coming."

At that, the flicker of warmth looked like it might actually become a smile. And as they stood there, just looking at one another, his gaze heated a good several degrees, before he cleared his throat and looked away.

Pull yourself together, Tilly, she said, choosing Eve's most unyielding big sisterly tone. *Ignore the flickers and the furrows and the warm tingles, as they mean exactly nothing.*

For if she'd stayed, those feelings would have faded over time. Surely. Or worse, fractured and turned to hurt. Perhaps they had been lucky, not to have had to go through that, not to have lived in her parents' footsteps after all.

"Shall we?" he said, motioning to the front doors of the château. *His* château.

"I guess so," she said.

Yes, she had come to help her sisters. But perhaps this trip would work twofold. Having met a handsome prince, she might finally face reality and let the fairy tale go.

Matilda got as far as the entrance hall before her feet stopped working. For there were châteaux and then there were *châteaux*. And the Château de Chaleur earned all its capitals.

From the pale mosaic floors to an elegantly curving three-story staircase, to the soaring ceilings bright with beautifully preserved frescoes and doors leading to rooms that hinted at more quiet luxury, it looked like something out of a Merchant Ivory film and smelled like history.

"You *live* here," she said, her voice sounding far, far away.

"This is my family home."

Turned out trying not to imagine what being married to the man might mean…was not as easy as she'd hoped.

Matilda reached out for a nearby chair, some gilded curlicued antique that had likely been in Henri's family for generations, and sat just before her knees gave way. Then she leaned over, slowly, till her head was between her knees.

"Lars," Henry—no, *Henri*—commanded, and Matilda saw a pair of very large black shoes lumber into her sight line. Though, next to Henri's sharp brown Oxfords they weren't much bigger at all. Okay, so if she was in the frame of mind to compare men's shoe sizes, then she was okay. "Have Celeste come down, *s'il vous plaît*," Henri murmured, his accent thickening. "Ms. Matilda is not well."

"I'm fine!" Matilda said, slowly sitting up and pushing her hair from her face. "It's probably delayed jet lag. And hunger. Where I'm from, we require more than a single *petit four* in our bellies before finding out our old…" She paused. "Old *friends* have their own castles."

She smiled up at Lurch—no, *Lars*—to prove that she was not falling apart. Though he looked as if he was far more comfortable dealing with über-cool princes than swooning farm girls.

"Sir?" Lars asked, looking to Henri, who was now frowning as if his brow furrows alone might save the planet.

"Lars," Boris chastised from his position watching Henri. *"Va trouver Celeste."*

"Ah, oui," said Lars before lumbering off.

While Matilda watched Henri watch her. His gaze had settled on her hair, making her wonder how crazy it looked. Or if it was some royal peccadillo. The royals she'd researched when first learning how to trace provenance of old letters, had certainly had some weird predilections. All that inbreeding.

"How were your parents related?" she asked.

Boris cleared his throat, bringing his fist to his mouth as if covering a cough.

While Henri's eyes narrowed, turning all bedroomy and beautiful and lit with mild outrage. "They were *not*. My father was a Raphael-Rossetti, born second in line to the throne of Chaleur. My mother was Italian, the granddaughter of a count."

"Cool," she said, thinking how *"the throne of Chaleur"* tripped off Henri's tongue like it was all so normal. Then she queried, "Was?"

Understanding her, Henri said, "They are both gone."

"Oh." So, he was an orphan. Just like her. "Mine too. My parents. My father only recently. My mother…several years ago."

She watched him, waiting for a flare of recognition, or discomfort at how he'd behaved, but he turned away.

"Boris," he said, "can you please check to see how Lars is getting on in finding Celeste?"

Boris nodded, turned on his heel, and left.

When Matilda placed her hands on her knees and pressed herself to standing, Henri moved in, his hand hovering below her elbow, in case she was still off-kilter. And when her gaze lifted to his, they were close. And alone. No wind and car noise, no curious gazes, no listening ears.

Was now the time to lay out her request? Find legal confirmation that their marriage was valid and hope he'd be amenable to keeping it that way for the next twelve months?

Perhaps. But instead, she found herself caught by that compelling, soulful, heart-achingly beautiful face.

"You've changed," she said, before she even felt the words coming. Her hand lifted, as if readying to trace her thumb along the deeper creases in his forehead.

"Matilda," he said, his jaw hard, his voice low, raw—

"Doth my eye deceive me?" a voice called from the top of the stairs.

Matilda flinched, and Henri's eyes drifted closed, before they both turned to find Andre, Henri's cousin, the enforcer of the cabbalistic rules of their Summer of Freedom, jogging down the staircase.

"Matilda?" he said, grinning as he reached the foyer floor.

"Hey, Andre."

He moved in, kissed her on both cheeks, then said, "If this was not so far beyond the realms of probability, I'd have thought my cousin tracked you down and brought you here to distract me from asking how his meeting with parliament went."

"Andre," Henri murmured, his voice deep with warning.

Andre's gaze sharpened as he took in Henri's hand, still hovering under Matilda's elbow. "She's not running away just yet. Are you?"

Ouch, thought Matilda.

Henri's hand dropped away and he took a step back.

"How on earth did you *finally* find us again," Andre asked.

"We found one another," she said, looking around him to catch Henri's eye. "On the street in Côte de Lapis."

"How lucky for us all." Andre's gaze swept to his cousin, the men sending coded messages with their eyes. Matilda knew because she and her sisters did it all the time.

A woman around Matilda's age, wearing a neat cream suit, elegant heels, blond hair pulled into a sleek low bun appeared silently a few feet behind the cousins. "Your Highness?"

"Celeste," said Henri, "this is Matilda. An old friend of Andre's."

Andre's expression turned incredulous.

"Oh," said Celeste, blinking at Andre, before fixating on Matilda. Then, "Welcome to le Château de Chaleur."

And Matilda found herself curtsying.

Andre burst into laughter. "Wrong one, darling."

Henri gave Andre one final dark look, said, *"Excusez-moi,"* then took Celeste to one side and spoke quietly while she listened intently.

Andre moved in beside Matilda. "So that's how we're going to play it."

"Play?"

"You're *my* friend, not his. For the best, I suppose. The last thing Henri needs right now is news of an old flame turning up on his doorstep. The royalists will be calling for babies, while the antimonarchists would have a field day."

She turned to him. "Antimonarchists?"
Babies?

Andre brushed it aside, his gaze hard on Henri and Celeste, as if trying to read their lips. Then he looked deep into her eyes, as if trying to ascertain her devious plans. "Why are you here, Matilda? Why now?"

She said nothing for it was Henri's business, not his, though Andre had always found it hard to separate the two.

"Are you are sticking with the *I didn't know who he really was* line?"

"Nobody knew anything," Matilda reminded him. "Thanks to you."

Andre blinked. "It was rather ingenious of me, though I still can't believe we pulled it off." He turned to face her. "What about since?"

"What about it?"

"Prince Augustus, our fiscally imbecilic brute of an uncle, abdicated not long after you disappeared into the ether. After which Henri's screwball father, Prince Marcel, took over. Far less subtle about the millions he stole from the realm. Still nothing?"

Matilda shook her head, while carefully storing away the precious morsels of Henri's life that she'd never known.

"Prince Marcel, Henri's father, died two years ago. Car accident. Drove off a cliff taking Henri's older brother, the heir, Pascal, with him. Our Henri has been Sovereign Prince ever since."

Matilda turned back to Henri, noting again the stiff shoulders, the perfect suit, the neat hair, the otherness that hovered around him like a cloud. With all that to contend with, no wonder he'd changed. No wonder he seemed so aloof.

"You ladies usually lap that stuff up," said Andre.

Matilda coughed out a laugh. "We ladies?"

Andre's gaze made it clear he was pushing buttons, looking to trip her up somehow.

Matilda crossed her arms. "Do you know where *I* live?"

His gaze flickered. "Australia, clearly, by the accent. Somewhere near Sydney?"

Matilda pulled out her phone, looked up a map app and found Garrison Downs. Then she pulled back, and back and back.

"That's Sydney," she said pointing at the east coast city. "And that," she said, dragging her finger dramatically, across thousands of miles of hostile land before poking a finger in the middle of South Australia, "is home."

Andre squinted. "Do you even have internet?"

"Of course, we have internet," she said.

And Andre shot her a victorious smile.

"Though it's unpredictable," she allowed. "Even then the news of the day revolves around stock prices, El Niño, broken fences, the new teacher in town. Not the ins and outs of teeny-tiny *lesser-known* European principalities."

Andre's eyes widened at her rebuff, clearly enjoying the fight. "Weren't you some kind of history buff?"

"My PhD would attest to that fact."

A flare of the nostrils, then a small tilt of the head in appreciation from Andre.

"Though my bent is handwritten letters. Collections thereof. Shove something of that ilk under my nose and my heart will go pitter-pat. Show me a gossip site starring young, hot, Euro royalty and I remain unmoved."

Andre shot a single eyebrow northward. "Unmoved? And yet your gaze keeps tracking a certain real live young, hot Euro royal even as we speak."

Matilda felt a flush of heat rush into her cheeks. Then she realised Henri was approaching, close enough to have heard Andre's attestation. Which had, no doubt, been Andre's intention.

"Is my cousin playing nice?" Henri asked, unable to mask the edge to his voice.

Matilda felt it scrape over her skin like a touch. "Why you need security when you have your cousin around, I'm not sure."

Henri's smile was quick, then it was gone. "He's much improved since you last met. And far too busy acting as my closest advisor to commit to permanent guard dog duties."

"Woof," Andre shot back. Then, sauntering away, lobbed a final velvet-wrapped grenade, "I hope to see you again, Matilda. Before you leave."

With the tip of his chin, Henri beckoned Matilda to follow him toward the stairs, and Matilda followed. On hollow legs. For it had been a lot.

"Celeste will show you to your room. Then find you something to eat. Multiple *petit fours*, if you desire. Whatever you need, we are at your disposal."

Desire. Petit fours. Whatever you need.

That burr in his voice. It muddled her a moment before she realised his intent.

"My *room*? No, no, I can book into a hotel." She looked around to find Celeste following at safe minimum distance. *"Un hotel...?"*

Celeste looked to Henri for instruction.

"Matilda," said Henri, his voice low, engaging, as he waited for her gaze to settle back on his.

And settle it did. Till she felt warm and loose under the focus of that pale hazel gaze.

"We have room here," said Henri. "Many rooms in fact. Most of which could do with company to fill them. We have...things to discuss."

The guy had no idea.

"Allow me to indulge you in the hospitality my home was built for."

"Mademoiselle?" Celeste encouraged.

As Matilda followed Celeste toward the stairs, she saw Henri's mouth open a fraction before he snapped it shut. About to suggest Matilda was a married *madame*?

But then he said, "Celeste, one more thing. Matilda has an aversion to food that wobbles."

Matilda laughed, delighting in the fact he'd picked up on her sassy little comment from earlier and held on to it. A frisson of warmth came over her at the possibility that beneath the cool, her Henry was in there somewhere still.

Not that she wanted that. Or needed it. Or found it in any way helpful.

While Celeste, clearly used to the vagaries of a royal household merely said, *"D'accord,"* and led the way.

Henri watched Matilda head up the stairs, stopping every step or two to ask Celeste a question about a painting, or a carving, or a fresco. While Celeste answered, in her usual efficient way.

"So," said Andre, sidling up to Henri, "the prodigal wife has returned."

"Must you?" Henri growled, glancing around to make sure they were still alone. For the château staff's job was to be loyal to Chaleur, not to him.

Andre grinned. "I must. After this turn of events, am I to assume this morning's meeting did not go ahead?"

Henri breathed out hard. "It did."

Andre sighed. "And how did our parliamentary friends take it when their prince told them that he would like them to consider undoing centuries' worth of governance by abolishing royal rule?"

"They were…surprised." Even while his predecessors had given them every reason to question the moral authority of the Raphael-Rossetti line, it was what they were used to.

"No," Andre deadpanned. "Really?"

"But they did listen." Henri faced his cousin. Needing him on board. "And they trusted my sincerity. They have agreed to put a poll into the field, couched language, careful. Gain some insight into how a referendum would pan out."

Andre shook his head. In dissent, or awe? Likely a mix of both. For while Andre took great pleasure in the trappings of their lifestyle, he had witnessed Henri's life up close. The scandal, the sorrow, a childhood spent at the mercy of their brutish uncle.

"On that," said Henri, "I was seen today, on the Côte de Lapis. A crowd gathered. You will be thrilled to know I engaged. Boris and Lars had to be talked down from karate chopping a dozen people."

"That is good news. And how did you cope?"

"Gingerly."

Andre laughed.

"There were questions. An undercurrent of concern. Are there rumours that I am unwell?"

Andre reached out and squeezed his shoulder. "You are their prince. They do not get to see as much of you as they would like. It worries them."

Henri shifted on his feet.

"Now, since one live grenade is not enough for you, *how is* she *here*?"

The timing of Matilda's arrival could not be more complicated. "She was sitting in Café du Couronne. Apparently, because *you* had mentioned, more than once, that we had spent a lot of time there."

"Ah," said Andre, running a hand up the back of his neck.

"Indeed. I brought her here, to keep her out of the public eye. At which point I blithely informed her who I am, waited for her to finish hyperventilating, then sent her upstairs. Now you're all caught up."

Andre glanced back up the stairs, where Matilda was now spinning slowly on the spot and looking at the fresco on the ceiling. "What happens now?"

What now, indeed?

When he and Matilda had met, he'd been a young man without a plan bar which book to read, which restaurant to eat clean, which town to hit next. Now, he spent his days reading parliamentary papers, speaking with industry experts, liaising with heads of state the world over, while also digging through piles of metaphorical rubble in the hopes of undoing the heinous mistakes of his forebears.

Matilda, on the other hand, looked fresh and vital and brimming with energy. As if she'd walked out of his life, then walked right back in.

At the top of the stairs Matilda looked back, saw him watching, and gave him a lift of her shoulders that said *How can any of this be real?*, then disappeared from view.

Henri breathed out hard.

"Wait," said Andre, "are those…? Yes, they are actual puppy dog eyes."

"Don't start."

"*I'm* not doing anything. You're the one who's going all gooey over the woman. Again. It must be pathological, considering how dark things went last time. If dear old Uncle Augustus hadn't abdicated in such a timely manner, thus dragging us both back to this godforsaken paradise, I fear what might have become of you."

While Andre's words were deliberately provocative, his gaze was concerned. For Andre had been there, keeping him from doing anything reckless, as he'd tried to understand where it had gone wrong.

"You are mistaken," said Henri. "Going 'gooey' is not my style."

"You honestly think that, don't you. Oh, cousin, you are so screwed."

Henri was concerned Andre might be right. But for a different reason entirely. For if anyone found out who she was and what had been, it could muddy the waters, making a true, people-led referendum moot.

He slapped Andre hard enough on the back to earn an *oof*. "Fun's over, we have work to do."

"*Mademoiselle,*" Celeste said, "your room."

Matilda thought the guest rooms in the Homestead were over-the-top, but this was something else.

A duck egg blue velvet lounge suite, white fur

rug, a fireplace as big as a bull. A series of French windows, draped in pale blue curtains, shed slivers of soft buttery light over the huge bed residing on a raised platform. Two sets of double doors she imagined led to walk-in wardrobes and an *en suite*. Though, considering her day thus far, they might just as well lead to Narnia, or outer space. Her suitcase with its cacophony of blue ribbons on the handle leaned in a corner of the room. Her handbag sat neatly on a stool, her laptop on a desk, charging.

"We hope this will suffice," Celeste said, deadpan.

"Suffice? I feel like I've walked into *The Princess Diaries.*"

"I found the second movie superior," Celeste insisted as she drew the curtains open, letting in great shafts of sunshine and a view over the mountains beyond that took Matilda's breath away.

Which was probably a good thing, as declaring herself a princess clearly contravened the promise she'd made to Rose to stay under the radar.

"Shall I have the kitchen send up…non-wobbly food?" Celeste asked.

Matilda shook her head. Then yawned the yawn of a person who'd been up for much of the past twenty-four hours, driving to and from airports, dragging luggage from one plane to another, while quietly panicking about the state of affairs she and her sisters were in.

"I think I'll just chill for a bit, if that's okay?"

Celeste nodded. "My personal number is on a card I've left on the desk. Dialling eleven on the phone by the bed will get you through to the kitchen. Dinner is at seven. If you head down the way you came up, someone will show you the way."

Once Celeste left, Matilda climbed onto the platform, lifted her tired arms to the side and let herself fall, landing on the bed with a bounce. The soft, sweetly scented blankets enveloped her in their cloudlike embrace.

A minute, she said to herself, yawning anew. *I'll just shut my eyes for a minute.*

CHAPTER THREE

HENRI SAT AT the head of the long dining table, cradling a fresh espresso, and attempting to read over a speech Andre wanted him to give to close off the Summer Festival celebrations. He'd talked his way out of the event the year before, but this year his excuses were falling on deaf ears.

He wasn't sure that the unexpected arrival of a surprise wife would cut it.

He put his phone face down. Impossible to concentrate when he'd spent much of the night wondering why she was there.

The possible reasons were many. His family history was rife with so many stories of secret babies and communicable diseases, even he could not remember them all, and he had been schooled in Chaleurian history till his fingers had bled. Literally.

The likeliest reason was that she had met someone and was there to ask him for a divorce.

Henri sipped his espresso without thinking,

wincing at the heat of it. Then, after a beat, downed the lot in one hit.

"Carefully, carefully, amore mio..." his mother's soft voice, a voice he'd not heard in over two decades, whispered into his ear. A voice that could not have been more different from the voice that had fostered his education after she'd died.

His uncle, Prince Augustus, a hand tight at his neck, eyes boring into Henri's as he commanded, "With strength and power, always."

"Hey."

Henri flinched at the sound, abhorring the fact that memories of his uncle could mess with his equilibrium still.

He looked up to find Matilda standing in the doorway, her hair loose and a little wild, her eyes crystal bright, her face soft with sleep. And despite the fact he'd spent much of the past several hours thinking of little but her, and how disruptive her arrival might yet be, there was no denying the slide of heat passing through him.

He brought a linen napkin to his mouth and pushed back his chair. "Good morning, Matilda."

"Sit, sit," she said, flapping a hand his way.

Unused to being given commands these days, he paused, then did as asked. "Join me."

"Are you sure?" She waved a hand over high-waisted jeans and a cropped T-shirt the same forget-me-not-blue of her eyes. "Most of my clothes are in dire need of a wash, and even then I didn't exactly pack for dining with royalty."

"I'm sure I could rustle up a spare tiara if that would make you more comfortable."

"So much more comfortable," she said with a smile.

After which they simply looked at one another, for far too long. Before Matilda bit her bottom lip and looked away. "On that, if someone could point the way to the laundry…"

"Let Celeste know. She'll get it sorted for you."

Matilda pointed one way, then another. "Do you not know where it is?"

Henri stalled. He was not entirely sure.

She reached out to grab the back of the chair at the far end of the table. "Do you remember, when we stayed in Sorrento, I had to teach you how to use a washer and dryer?"

He remembered watching her take charge, explaining the steps to him with exaggerated simplicity. No one had ever treated him with such a lack of deference. It had been a revelation.

"I assumed you were spoiled," Matilda went on. "Not, you know, a prince."

"One often comes with the other."

Matilda rocked the chair on its back legs. "I've seen enough movies to know that if I sit here, we'll come unstuck when one of us needs the other to pass the salt."

It was also, according to custom, where his wife would sit.

He motioned to the chair perpendicular to his. "Excellent salt-passing distance."

She moved down the length of the table, her hand running over the top of each chair, her gaze wandering about the room. "Anyone else joining us?"

Henri shook his head.

At one point in his childhood, the château had been filled with family. Noise. Life. For Prince Augustus and his wife, upon discovering they could not have children of their own, had opened the palace to Henri's family, and Andre's, and a dozen more distant cousins. Bar Andre, the rest were now gone—having moved as far away from Augustus and his pedagogy as possible.

Now it was a far quieter place.

Matilda sat, her knees lifting as her feet balanced on her toes. Then she asked, "So is it Henry or *Henri*?"

Her question appeared innocuous, but he saw the wound in her eyes. As if all that they had done in the name of being young and free had bruised them both in the end.

"I have gone by both. Henry, mostly, while studying."

"Where did you study?" she asked, her voice lilting, as if hungry to know more.

"Political science at the Sorbonne. MBA via the London School of Economics."

"That tracks. And *Henri*?"

"My birth name."

"Gallo?"

"My mother's maiden name. By Chaleurian law, while it appears on my birth certificate it is not an official part of my title."

She absorbed the information like a sponge. Then smiled. The clouds clearing. And he felt the same within his chest. An easing. A lifting. A lightness he'd not felt in quite some time.

Carefully, carefully.

She nodded. "Well, your place is pretty nice, *Henri*."

Henri felt his mouth tug at the corner. "We like it."

"And that bed of yours was amazing. I mean *my* bed. The one you put me in—*Celeste* put me in. The *sheets* are top-notch. And the blankets are so fluffy. And…" She stopped, took a breath.

"The pillows?" he asked, helpfully.

Her eyes found his, sparkled. "Meh."

He laughed. Loudly. Enough that he surprised even himself.

And Matilda's face altered in the most stunning way, her cheeks pinking, her eyes softening, as if his laughter was already her very favourite part of the day.

"So how does it work?" she asked, leaning her

elbow on the table and looking up at him from beneath what seemed like a thousand eyelashes. "Your princeliness?"

"Do you mean politically?" he asked. "Or do I brush my hair a hundred times before bed?"

Her bark of laughter was infectious. "The former. For starters."

"We are a monarchical sovereign state, which means, as Sovereign Prince, I am head of state."

"Go, you."

"Mmm, but it's not because I have the best ideas, or the brightest mind, or the most empathetic nature, but because of who my father was, and his father before him."

"Mmm," she parroted. "So its actual work, then. Not just ribbon-cutting ceremonies, and smashing bottles of bubbly on the sides of ships?"

"I leave that to Andre."

That earned him another laugh. All husky and rich and true. Only the moment the sound hit him, he knew it had been a mistake. Encouraging it. Encouraging her.

For while much had happened since they'd last seen one another, to hone him, to inure him to outside forces, this woman had once upon a time proven she had the power to cut him to shreds.

"Are you hungry?" Henri asked, refocusing. One of the waitstaff waiting in the wing stepped off his mark in preparation.

"Nope. Eaten already." She mimed dialling a

phone. "Someone brought me French toast, berries, yoghurt, fresh squeezed orange juice. No Vegemite, alas, but I can forgive that." Then, "I wasn't aware that this was an option."

"This?"

"Eating here," she said simply, "with you."

He felt a tingle in the back of his head, more in the tips of his fingers, as if his blood momentarily forgot where it was meant to be. Then a waiter cleared his throat. Henri had completely forgotten the man was there.

Which was when he saw it. Not on her left hand, where he had placed it that long-ago night, but on her right. His mother's ring. She had brought it with her. Along with a plan to give it back? Surely she'd not worn it all these years. Both thoughts turned his insides to knots. Meaning the sooner he got to the bottom of why she was there, the better.

"How are you on the water?" he asked, as he pressed back his chair.

"I'm Australian, Henri. We are two-thirds water."

Halfway to standing, Henri found himself coughing out another laugh. The feeling was both strange and addictive. "Matilda, we are all two-thirds water."

"Well, what do you know?" she said, halfway to standing herself. "I'm more similar to royalty than I ever knew."

* * *

"Henry!" Matilda laughed as his yacht tore across the crystalline surface of Lac d'Hiver, the private, near perfect circle of mountain water at the rear of the château. "This is spectacular!"

She glanced back at him, her cheeks pink from the sun and wind, her eyes bluer, if possible, than the famously blue water below.

"Sorry, *Henri*," she said, mirroring his accent, and adding a little flair just to rub it in. "Or should I call you 'Your Highness'?"

"Henri is fine."

When she had first called him Henry, over Henri, he'd not corrected her. But it hadn't been long before he'd longed to hear her call him by his proper name. For her to know him for who he truly was. It was Andre who had convinced him to stick to their rules. Insisted, in fact, reminding him the rules that had been put into place to protect *him*. To give him the freedom he'd so craved.

But that was all so long ago.

Henri eased back on the throttle, hand resting loosely on the wheel. "Matilda," he said.

Finger trailing through the water as they drifted, she looked up.

"Perhaps now is a good time to tell me why you are here."

"Of course," she said. Her cropped T-shirt lifted to flash a swathe of tanned skin as she settled back in her seat, and the chipped bronze polish on her bare foot poked out the bottom of her too-long jeans.

Then she closed her eyes, held out both hands as if steadying herself, and said, "I know you're busy, but I hope you can indulge me while I give you some background. Some context to what I'm about to ask."

Her eyes lifted to his. The words *for despite who we once were, we know nothing about one another, not really* remained unsaid.

She started with her sisters, Rose and Evelyn. Growing up together on a cattle station in the middle of the Outback. She spoke of her mother, Rosamund. How close they had been, how her mother was the reason why she'd travelled. How deeply the shock of her mother's death had affected them all.

She paused a moment then, as if waiting for him to say something.

But then she moved on to her father. "A little under two months ago, he was hit by a widow-maker—the falling branch from a gum tree—while mustering. He seemed okay afterwards. Bumps and bruises, aches and pains, but he was tough. Unstoppable. Until he wasn't. He collapsed one day, in the kitchen. Rose was out, so it fell on me. We were in the helicopter, heading to the local hospital, when he..." She swallowed. "Internal bleeding. A lacerated spleen. There was nothing they could do."

She stopped, then sat forward, her head in her hands.

And something shifted inside of Henri. Like a landslide, shearing away some great layer of self-protection. He reached for her, his fingers hovering midair. But no.

The best he could do was sympathise. "I'm so sorry that you went through that."

"It's fine," she said, sitting up, breathing through her nose, shaking her head. "It's okay. I'm okay."

And he saw her tuck her sorrow away, call up a smile, and present as if all *was* fine. A move that came too easily, as if pretending, for someone else's sake, was a cloak she had donned many times.

His uncle's words, *"Never show weakness. Never show pain,"* reverberated in his head, and he bucked against it so hard he pulled a muscle in his chest.

"I understand the impulse," he said, his voice overloud to drown out his uncle's voice, "to want to appear as if everything is fine. But you do not have to pretend with me."

Her surprised gaze found his. Then in the next moment she seemed to crumble, becoming untethered, as if she'd been holding so much in for so long.

"I…" She licked her lips. "It's been weeks now, but I still keep expecting to hear the thwack of the back door, his three-toned whistle, the scrape of his boots on the polished wood floors. And—even though she's been gone several years now—I find myself expecting my mother's voice too, telling Dad to take off his shoes before she takes them off for him."

She took a deep breath, then thumped a fist against her chest. "I had no idea that was sitting, right here." Then, "Likely because there's so much more taking up space right now. All of which started upon the reading of his will."

After that, she told him the rest of her story in one freewheeling gulp.

The revelation of an affair. A secret sister. A century-old poker game. A neighbourly feud. And a wildly problematic stipulation as to the legitimacy of any female inheritance that did its best to out-dismay the stranger restrictions found in the Chaleurian rules of succession.

"My sister," she said, "Rose, has clammed up. Eve is furious, and thoroughly disconnected. Ana is like a deer in the headlights. While I'm… I'm mostly confused. Knowing him, and my mum, and how they were together—they were so tight. So loving. If they, who appeared to have the best marriage, nearly imploded, and so spectacularly, what hope is there for the rest of us?"

Her gaze connected with his then. Swirling with pain and shock and longing. Meaning it took a moment to sift through her story to find the point that truly affected him.

"You and your sisters, must be married, by…"

"The end of May, next year."

"Or your lands will be given back to the family who owned them generations ago."

"Correct. I have been trying to find a legal loophole that makes it redundant, while also being quiet about the whole thing, as the less people know the better. But we aren't having much luck. Meaning we have to start looking at Plan B."

Henri's throat was as dry as an autumn leaf, his voice crackling, as he clarified, "You wish to know whether we are, in fact, married."

"I do," she blurted. Then seemed to realise the words she'd chosen, and a pulse began beating in her neck.

He felt it too, a rise in temperature, a siren call back to those golden days and decadent nights. "And if we are legally married, you would ask that we remain that way, until such a date that your portion of the condition is satisfied."

She breathed out a *Yes*.

His response ought to have been an instant *No*.

If word got out that he, a prince in want of an heir, had married in secret years ago, royal detractors would have a field day. If word got out that he was engaged in a *fake* marriage, it would have the same outcome. It would weaken his position, or in the very least make it appear as if he put his own needs above the needs of the country. Which could not be further from the truth.

Though, instead of saying any of that, Henri watched Matilda's thumb twirl the ring on her right hand, his mother's ring, around and around, as if she was *used* to it being there.

And found himself saying, "What do your sisters think of your plan?"

"They don't know."

"That you are here?"

"They don't know about you."

His gaze whipped back to hers.

He had thought himself inured to the cut of a savage truth, his uncle having burnished his heirs with such methods until they shone. It seemed that this woman had power over him still.

Henri placed a hand on the throttle, turned the yacht and started the journey back to shore.

"I couldn't tell them," Matilda said, carefully manoeuvring her way up the boat till she took the seat next to his. "When I got home, Mum was in a coma, and she never came out. Our family was in disarray. Then it only became harder and harder to bring it up. Until it was just easier to forget it ever happened."

Henri pressed the throttle harder.

"Tell me it hasn't been the same for you," she said, her voice lifting to combat the roar of the engine.

Henri's jaw tightened. For she was right. The weeks and months right after were a daze to him now. But time healed. Patched over old wounds until they became no more than a scar.

"It seems a lot to ask of you all," he said, changing tack. "To make that kind of sacrifice for the sake of a plot of land. Would it not be easier to refuse. To start afresh?"

Matilda reared back. "How would you feel if you were told that you were to lose the château? Off you go, find a new job, somewhere else to sleep. Thanks for nothing."

Matilda had no idea how close she was to touching on what had once upon a time been his dream. That the summer they'd met he had put it behind him, wanting a different life. Only to be pulled back in.

"Do you believe that we are married?"

"I would err on the side of yes. But in actuality, I do not know for sure."

She nodded. "No matter what happens next, can you agree that we *need* to find out for sure?"

She was right. Their marriage was out there, an anvil over his head. The truth *would* out, and while he would not lie, if there was some way that he could control the messaging, it might not upend everything he was trying to achieve.

"I have one condition," he said.

Matilda's eyes widened. Before she collected

herself. Then, to cut the tension, she shivered and said, "That word."

And Henri's smile came from nowhere. It was a magic trick, her ability to pull that out of him when he least expected it.

"A consideration, then. While your situation is time sensitive, mine is sensitive in other ways."

"The prince thing."

"The prince thing."

How to put this?

"I have worked hard to let my people know that I can be trusted to put their interests ahead of my own. If news that I had been keeping a royal bride from them were to get out, it would be difficult to roll back."

The press, parliament, the people would all rightly be wondering. Was subterfuge simply in the Raphael-Rossetti blood? The fact that he was entertaining this at all sat ill within him. But what was he to do? Especially when discretion was important to her too.

"Whatever you need from me," said Matilda, "I will do."

Henri's eyebrow lifted of its own volition.

While Matilda blushed to her roots. "And by *that*, I mean, what steps do you believe we should take next?"

The dock grew larger as they approached. Henri slowed the boat right down, giving him a moment to collate his thoughts. "Allow me to

find a way to *quietly* find the legal documents
we require. Until then, no promises, no plans."

Matilda nodded. "Totally fair. And what shall
I do until then?"

"That's entirely up to you. That said, you have
arrived here at rather a pivotal moment, politically. So having you out of the public eye would
be my preference."

"Henri," she said, leaning in to nudge her shoulder against his. "Are you asking me to stay?"

"Yes, Matilda, I am asking you to stay. So that
you might stay under the radar."

"First Rose, then you. Why do people think
I'm going to go about the place announcing myself. Hi! I'm Matilda! Secretly married to your
prince!"

Henri glanced toward the deck where Boris
and Lars were walking down the stone steps,
readying to collect him. And only just out of
hearing range. This was going to be a hardship
on many levels.

"Will you stay?"

She looked over his shoulder toward the château, the morning sun picking up hints of peach
in the stone, making it appear as if it glowed, and
she, with an long-suffering sigh, said, "If I must."

"Then it's settled."

"It's settled." Matilda said, smiling at him as
if they were now in this thing together.

While Henri focused on getting the boat away

without a scratch, rather than the ripples of warmth
spreading through him at the knowledge she
wasn't leaving.

Not yet.

Carefully, carefully.

CHAPTER FOUR

IT WAS LATE the next afternoon before Henri was able to even think about how he might go about unearthing the validity of a marriage in a manner that could keep the search quiet.

He'd spent the hours in between as per usual, strapped to his office chair. On the phone to the Minister for Agriculture, who was concerned about predictions of a colder than normal winter. Then the chair of the Royal Opera, for which he was patron, wondering when he might actually attend an event. After which he'd taken part in an online video chat with a classroom of second graders from the local Chaleurian Charter School and had stumbled over the question, "What do you love most about being a prince?"

This, right on the heels of Minister of State letting him know, in sombre tones, that an anonymous poll had been put into the field; testing the waters as to which way a referendum regarding the future of the royal house of Chaleur might sway.

Stretching out tight shoulders, he moved to the

window of his first-floor office to find Matilda sitting at a table in the rose garden below.

Snacks and coffee within reach, it was a miracle she didn't fall off the chair, the way she sat with one foot on the seat, arm wrapped about her knee, as she tapped away at her laptop.

He lifted a hand to his chest when he felt a strange tightness take hold.

"Why so glum?"

Henri looked to his side to find his cousin had finally deigned to join him, after being summoned a good half hour earlier.

When he realised Andre was mimicking his stance—all stiff shoulders and pinched face— Henri let his hands unclasp. "I am glum due to the fact I need at least forty-eight hours in every day if I have any hope of restoring order to this house."

"That all?" Andre asked after a long beat.

For his simple question had apparently unlocked a wave of frustration in Henri. Matilda, now walking barefoot through the grass, and collecting fallen rose petals, had no doubt loosened the lid.

"I cannot remember the last time I read for pleasure, enjoyed a leisurely glass of wine, took a drive for no reason other than wishing it." The boat ride the day before had come close, after which he'd been playing catch-up all day.

"You are aware," said Andre, giving him a side-eye, "that the only one putting such pressure on yourself is you? If you really wanted to find time to do those things, you would. Or you could halve your workload by nabbing yourself a princess. Oh, wait!"

Henri did not dignify that with a response.

"On that note, I see *she's* still here."

"*She* is staying for a short while."

"How long?"

"No end date has been determined."

"Not that that's stopped her before."

Henri's eye twitched. "Tell me again why I allow you to walk about the place, unfettered? As prince I could, by law, have you beheaded."

"You indulge me because I am endearing as hell. And since I too was raised under the regime of Prince Augustus the Beloved Brute, I alone understand your occasional twitches are psychosomatic and not reason to call the royal doctor."

"There is that."

The cousins stood silent for a few moments, watching Matilda, who was now on her phone— her movements animated, her smile wide.

"Look at her out there," Andre mused, "pacing a route. Like a caged cat."

Henri flinched at Andre's choice of words, then turned away from the view. "I called you here as I need you to do something for me."

"I will not write down the Netflix password

again. Put a note in your phone like a normal person."

"I need you to find official record of my marriage to Matilda."

Andre's nostrils flared, but other than that, he did not react at all. He had been there that night. The lone witness to the event bar the yacht captain who, from memory, had limited English. And in the weeks and months after. When Henri had feared for her, longed for her, and cursed her very existence.

"You understand why I am asking this of you, and you alone. Why it needs to be done with subtlety and finesse. Whatever information you find must be unimpeachable. Can you do that for me?"

Andre waited a beat, then nodded. And that was that. For all that his cousin appeared the definition of imperious indolence, Henri knew why. To combat the darker parts of their childhood, Henri had shuttered himself behind physical and metaphorical walls. Andre had chosen snark.

"May I ask why now?"

"You may ask, but I cannot say." It was Matilda's story to share, not his. Even with Andre.

"Should I worry?"

"You will, even if I command you not to."

Andre's gaze flickered, as if surprised Henri had realised that about him.

"Make it a priority," Henri said, with gentle command.

Andre nodded, knocked twice on the door-frame, then left.

Henri turned back to the window to find Matilda looking up, her phone cradled in her hand. She blinked when they made eye contact and looked away, before looking back, as if she'd been caught watching him.

He lifted his hand in a wave. She waved back, before pointing up, asking if she might join him.

And while the backlog of work beckoned from his desk, he nodded.

The twist in his chest loosened when she smiled broadly, jogged to the table to collect her things, then disappeared inside.

Henri found himself glad Andre had already left the room.

Matilda—still getting used to the servants who seemed to lurk in doorways in this place, like security in a museum—muffled a scream when Celeste appeared from nowhere.

"May I help you, Ms. Matilda?"

"Ah, well I'm just heading up to see Henri. Prince Henri. His Royal…you know. He invited me up."

Good grief. Could she be any more obvious? Or less sophisticated?

Funny how she'd forgotten that side of things in the intervening years—the times she'd wondered how she, a bumptious farm girl with a penchant for gum boots and denim overalls, had ended up in their glittering circle.

Then she'd catch Henri's eye and she'd know exactly why she was there.

"He's in the room just above?" she said, twirling a finger above her head, then spinning a half turn.

"*Oui*, His Highness is in his office," said Celeste. "I can show you the way."

At which point a maid appeared, again from nowhere, asking if she could take the coffee and plate Matilda was juggling. Matilda handed them off gratefully, no clue as to whether they were family heirlooms or from some IKEA collection the kitchen used for non-royal guests.

If only they knew, a cheeky voice popped up in the back of her head. Before a shiver of discomfort wobbled through her, and she told the voice to shush.

Following Celeste, Matilda used one hand to send a quick message to Eve. Giving her an update on her phone call she'd just had with Rose. Not that Eve would respond, but at least she might feel part of things still. While frustrating, Matilda understood. It was hard on all of them.

Which was why she had to make this work.

Rose had to know something was up, for Matilda had not been able to stop peppering her with questions about home and telling Rose how amazing she was.

It was either that, or tell her about the rose garden, a near twin to their mother's, or the fairy-tale castle she had promised not to leave. Or Henri. Standing in the window above, like something out of one of the romance novels Eve used to read. All broad and distinguished and broody and gorgeous. The beautiful boy now honed, sharpened, perfected over time.

But there was still no point in getting Rose excited—or, more likely, furious—that she had gone rogue, until she had answers. Much like prepping a research paper for peer review, she needed to be fully equipped to stand by her premise. Whatever that turned out to be.

Laptop under her arm, she jogged up the stairs after Celeste.

That was one positive of the day. She'd woken with an idea for a chapter in the book she was working on. And outside in that beautiful soft sunlight, in the forest-fresh air, she'd drafted the first chapter.

Celeste glanced back to make sure she was keeping up.

"Sorry, daydreaming."

Celeste nodded, while looking as if she'd never daydreamed in her life.

Matilda wondered what Celeste thought of her—"Andre's friend," who had spent no time with Andre at all.

Unless that was some kind of code. Did Henri

often have women come to stay? It would be more of a shock if he did not. For if he was not atop some list of eligible royals, she'd eat her skirt.

She had zero excuse for the thought to curdle inside of her, considering how things had ended between them. But the idea of him looking longingly into someone's eyes, reading them poetry, or…

Nope. Not going there. Draw a line under it and move on.

Anyway, it just didn't feel as if guests were commonplace. The château felt quiet. The ivy climbing the long stone wall leading to the big creaky gate, the surfaces clean as a whistle but with a ghostly sense of unstirred dust. As if it had once been a bustling home but was currently in an era of repose.

Celeste stopped outside an imposing double door, knocked three times, waited a beat, then opened the door.

Matilda poked her head in to find Henri sitting behind a large desk, on the phone. He held up a staying hand, indicating he'd just be a minute.

She nodded, put her phone and laptop on a coffee table near a comfortable-looking couch, then went stickybeaking, taking in the artwork, the books on the shelves, the detritus. For *this* room was lived in.

Is this the real him? she wondered, picking up

a throw cushion that had fallen to the floor and tossing it onto a leather couch.

The Henri beneath the impossibly perfect exterior. A man who worked hard, took on too much, and thought little of the visuals.

"Matilda?"

She looked up to find Henri moving from behind his desk in his usual perfectly cut suit pants clinging to strong thighs, top button of his shirt undone, shirtsleeves rolled up to his elbows, veins roping down his beautiful forearms.

Her heart leaped as he neared, then panted like a happy puppy. She told it to sit. Stay. Leave.

Henri said, "Apologies if I've been unavailable."

She waved a hand his way. "I get it. You did mention that you have a country to run, and that you are all-powerful."

A beat slunk by. "I'm not sure those were the exact words I used."

"No?"

He slid hands into the pockets of his suit pants then, and she did not look down. Knowing what she was missing, she honestly deserved a medal.

"I trust Celeste has given you ideas of places you can visit within the grounds."

"Conservatory, orangery, rose garden, chapel. This place is like something out of a really well-funded historical TV drama."

"You've seen it all?" he asked, eyebrows lifting.

She had. Sitting still for long was not her thing.

"I even found the laundry. I can show you where it is?"

She pointed to the door, but instead he leaned back against his desk, crossed his feet at the ankle, and basically looked ready for GQ to step in and start snapping cover photos.

"What were you working on?" He motioned his chin to her discarded laptop.

She opened her mouth to mention the book, but found she wasn't yet ready to talk about it. It was at that tenuous it-might-all-dissolve-away-if-she-described-it-wrong point. And besides the subject matter was a little too close to home.

So she sidestepped to work she'd done the night before. "A letter. Possibly quite important, historically."

His brow furrowed and she had to reach out a hand in case her knees went out from under her.

"You were *writing* a letter?"

"Authenticating." She sat on the arm of the couch, just in case his brow furrowed again. "I have a PhD in art history. Authenticating hand-written letters is my niche."

"Fascinating."

She smiled, remembering he was a history buff too. The way he'd speak about painters and architects and political figures, the way he'd never rush through a museum, absorbing every display, his arm around her shoulder, hers wrapped around his waist, his voice rumbling from his chest to hers as he read every plaque, had been like catnip.

Now, looking around this place, she understood why.

"What kind of letter?" he asked, and the burr in his voice made her wonder if he was remembering the same.

She paused a moment before saying, "Well, it's a love letter, actually. For that is my *niche* niche."

"Of course, it is," he murmured.

Or maybe she'd imagined it. For the way his eyes remained on hers had her blood rushing behind her ears. Had her remembering lying with her head on his chest as he'd read to her from the book she'd bought him in Paris, her fingers trailing over the hard ridges of his torso, his trailing down her spine, lower.

And the longer his gaze hooked hers, the more she felt it. The undercurrent of heat. Of attraction. Still bubbling away between them. Which was something she honestly hadn't expected.

Yes, they had once upon a time been everything to one another. But she'd been so young, so green, and the way things had ended between them had hurt, deeply. Add her dad's affair to the mix and the very last thing she could put her faith in was *feelings*.

But there it was. That pulsing magnetic pull. And she knew it was tugging both ways.

Matilda pushed off the chair and moved around

the other side of his desk and pretended to look out the window. "Any news on the…thing we are trying to find news on?"

"Sorry," he said, moving to stand near her, but far enough away she was sure he was also keen on keeping minimum safe distance.

He ran a hand up the back of his neck, a classic stressed Henri move. "I know you must want answers as fast as possible so that you can…do whatever else you might wish to do while here."

"I have nowhere else I need to be." She made the mistake of looking at him as she said it and felt a kick of heat hit so hard she rocked on her feet.

"But you're right," she said, "the sooner it's all sorted, the better. I just spoke to Rose and she had a meeting with the family lawyer. Stubborn old goat is not being the slightest bit helpful."

"Time for a new family lawyer?"

"I did suggest that. Rose shot me down. She can wrangle a brumby and fly a helicopter, but she is too nice for her own good."

"Unlike you?" he asked, and when she looked to him again, it was clear he was baiting her. That whatever was humming between them he was leaning into, not away from.

"Are you kidding?" she said, "I'm a total dream."

"That so?"

So much for trying to cool things down. "Yep.

My role is the family conciliator. I am in charge of general harmony. I am sunshine and light."

"Why is that?"

She readied for a comeback but nothing came to her. For while she wasn't a big fan of confrontation, and she honestly wanted everyone to be happy, the why of it was unclear.

Henri threw her a bone. "Everyone called my older brother, Pascal, a chip off the old block, but where my father was a loose cannon, Pascal was, at heart, shy."

His brow furrowed, but not in a seductive way so much as a thoughtful way. Not that her libido was all that adept at differentiating.

"I wonder," said Henri, "if he too believed that he was fulfilling a role. Only it was the one written for him by our father, rather than the one he might have wanted for himself." When he ran a hand up the back of his neck that time, he left it there, gripping hard.

Family, she thought. *Can't live with them but love them to death.*

"And you?" she asked. When he didn't answer, she extrapolated. "If you say he lived down to people's expectations, did that mean you were expected to make up for him?"

His gaze slid back to hers, cynicism warring with scepticism behind his pale hazel eyes. And it hit her that she'd found out more about his childhood, his life, about what made him *him* in a five-minute conversation than she had the entire time they'd been together.

"We each of us contain multitudes," she said, paraphrasing Whitman, one of Henri's favourites, back in the day.

"It seems that we do," he said, his voice rough as their eyes caught and held.

Again. It had become a bit of a habit. One she could not deny felt wonderful. Invigorating. Empowering. And terrifying. For she'd never felt with another man the way she felt when she was with him.

Right when she was about to source a bucket of cold water in which to dunk her head, Henri stepped back. Turned away. And the spell splintered.

Though the aftereffect remained, like fireflies just under her skin.

"Hungry?" he asked.

"Famished," she admitted.

He picked up the phone, politely asked for a selection of sandwiches, cheeses, and petit fours to be delivered to his office.

"Nothing that wobbles," he noted.

And Matilda's heart took a big tumble. Which was a very foolish thing for it to do. For she had been there once before, deeply, forever his. And when she'd been swept up in the most terrible moment of her life, he'd not followed. Not checked on her. He'd simply cut her loose.

So yes, protecting her heart was a fantastic idea. As the time would soon come when they would have to say goodbye, only this time it would be forever.

Henri's phone beeped as he was washing shaving foam from his cheeks the next morning. Then it beeped again. And again.

He ignored it. Needing to finish at least one job semi-well, even if it was only shaving his face.

There was also the fact that he was hoping to make it to breakfast, as Matilda had asked, in her roundabout way, what time he normally ate, as it might be nice to cross paths.

Having company—bar Andre and Celeste or Boris and Lars hovering on the periphery—was something he had wilfully not sought out for some time. His role too important to allow for distractions. Having Matilda nearby hadn't been as disquieting as he'd thought it would be. In fact, there had been a kind of emphatic energy coursing through him the rest of the afternoon.

He'd also picked up on the fact that Matilda was used to having people around. Her sister, station hands, stable masters, seasonal staff, their housekeeper, Lindy. And her dad, not long lost. He wanted her to feel comfortable while there. Not, how had Andre put it? Like a caged cat.

His phone beeped again, three times in quick succession.

He checked quickly, his throat closing up when he saw Andre had sent a number of links to local news articles. Had someone read between the lines of the tele poll? Had news of a possible referendum been uncovered? Or had Matilda's arrival on the street the day before found traction?

As it turned out, it was none of the above. The overarching headline—Will Prince Henri Show His Face at the Summer Festival?

Henri's thumb hovered over the phone, a scathing response at the ready, but he called his cousin instead.

"Are you serious?" he growled.

"Thought you'd like to know your people miss you."

"I thought I made it clear what your priority needed to be." His marriage and its validity.

"That you did, cousin," said Andre. "And yet… the Summer Festival calls."

Henri thought back to the kindly response of the people on the street in Côte de Lapis. In his effort to not appear a show pony like his father, or remind them of the pain his uncle had caused, was it *possible* he'd gone too far the other way?

Then he remembered the piles of work on his desk, some of which he'd left half done while falling asleep late the night before. The referendum, which he might be pulling on them any day now. And wondered how on earth he could fit in an appearance for appearance's sake.

Matilda would enjoy it, he thought.

"Take Matilda," Andre said, reading his damn mind. "She's a venturesome sort. She'd love it."

"I can't *take* her."

"Too late for that."

Henri's unimpressed pause was answer enough.

"Look," said Andre, his tone placating, "you just...you need to get out of your own head. And if that means *getting out*, in general, then I, as your closest adviser and most stylish friend, encourage you to consider it."

Henri took a deep breath and thought back to the festivals of his youth. A welcome address. Judging a contest of some sort. Answering questions no more pressing than *"What do you enjoy most about being a prince?"*

But if he did let Matilda tag along, would their attraction be as blindingly obvious as it had felt in his office the day before? Like an arc of electricity connecting them. Making it impossible for him to keep his gaze from her.

He put the phone on speaker and dropped his hands to the sink. "This is not the time for parties and fun, Andre. This is my opportunity to make a difference. To fix mistakes. To give the people a real say in their futures."

"Henri," Andre said, sounding exasperated, "I have never heard someone say anything that made me more sure *they* were in need of parties and fun. Or perhaps some snuggle time with someone they found appealing."

"Moving on."

"As you wish."

"Do you have news? Regards—"

"Operation Is Henri Married?"

"Perhaps something with a little more tact."

"Noted. Nothing as yet, but I am on the case. Fingers in pies. Ears to the ground."

"And you are being careful."

"I was considering buying a trench coat."

Sighing, then patting his face with a towel, Henri said, "Just do what you need to do. Only quicker." With that he hung up.

Catching his own gaze in the mirror, he allowed himself a moment to wonder what *she* saw. *"You have changed,"* she'd said. And he had. In many ways.

In others, particularly those pertaining to her, it seemed he had not. For the more time he spent with her, the more he recognised the discomfort within him as a deep, primal longing. As if they were drawn to one another like twin storms, their edges bussing and bumping, waiting for the moment they hit at just the right angle and—

Henri closed his eyes against the image that came next.

Once he'd collected himself, he wiped his jaw, threw the towel to the sink and strode into his bedroom, where he dressed himself before heading straight to his office.

She could breakfast without him. For hiding the way they sparked off of one another from the staff would only become harder the more time they spent together. And it was not his job to make her feel at home.

For this was not her home. Oftentimes, he struggled to feel as if it was his. And they had agreed to a holding pattern.

No promises, no plans.

CHAPTER FIVE

"WHAT'S ON THE calendar for tomorrow?" Matilda asked that evening, while curled up on a chair in Henri's office.

Henri looked at her in the gilt mirror that had been brought in as his tailor fussed with the collar of a new suit.

Despite having avoided her at breakfast, she had found him once again at lunchtime. Knocking three times on his office, opening the door, then padding inside, the kitchen staff following, bringing a variation on the food they'd eaten together the day before.

Only this time, once they'd eaten and had fallen into a conversation about their respective school days—hers at a local country primary school with thirty children and two teachers, and his homeschooled by a retired professor with the personality of a taxidermised bug—she'd curled up on a couch in the corner with her laptop, humming under her breath as she continued working on her "letters and other things" while he worked at his desk.

Anytime he'd looked up from his work to find Matilda there, watching him, before shooting him a quick smile and going back to her work, his lack of progress felt less like he was drowning.

In the reflection in the mirror he watched her curious eyes follow as the tailor measured his inseam, tracing the run of the tape down his leg and back up again. Stopping to stare at his backside.

"Calendar?" he repeated. And when her eyes snapped to his, she had the grace to blush.

"Well," said Matilda, "I was thinking you must be dying to get out of here. And you shouldn't have to stay in on my account."

"There are options, certainly," said Celeste, who was standing to one side, overseeing the tailor's work. "If His Highness wishes to undertake them."

His Highness did not. Which Celeste knew all too well. He shot her a glance but she did not meet his eye, making him wonder how much time Andre had spent in her ear, rather than doing what needed to be done to find his damn marriage license.

"Ooh," said Matilda. "Options sound exciting. Maybe I could come along. I'd stay out of the way, of course. Shadow Celeste, as she shadows you. See a true day in the life of Prince Henri Gaultier Raphael-Rossetti. Assuming, that is," said Matilda, moving on the chair so that her legs swung from one side to the other, a move so sinuous, Henri had to grit his teeth and think of England, "that you do more than frown at paperwork, sign off on laws that change people's lives, and charm the masses in accidental beachside parades."

Henri lifted an eyebrow at her take on his position.

While he chose not to be the kind of royal to cut the ribbon on any new luxury car superstore, unlike his father, for Matilda, being stuck in a castle was clearly constrictive.

Henri, now duly triggered, took the foot off his own back. And looked to Celeste. "Options, you say?"

Celeste blinked, experienced what looked to be a moment of catatonia, then pulled up her phone and began flicking madly through the thing.

"Invitations that have been vetted by Boris include...a children's hospital visit. A science lab which has just had a breakthrough in dementia treatment. It's National Tree Planting Week—"

As Celeste went through the surprisingly long list of groups who had invited him to visit, Henri heard Andre's voice in the back of his head saying, *The only one putting such pressure on yourself is you. You could halve your workload by nabbing yourself a princess.*

His gaze shifted back to Matilda, as it was wont to do, to find her smiling at Celeste. And he let himself wonder.

For *no promises, no plans* did not mean Henri was not constantly contemplating what might come next. If the marriage was valid, Matilda could have her marriage certificate, and his country could have its princess.

But then there was the referendum to consider. If it went ahead, and the people chose to move forward in a new way, it would take time, years perhaps, before the dismantlement of generations of royal rule was complete.

Only then would his life be his own. Not for a summer, but forevermore.

Henri felt the tug of the tailor's hand against his calf. Once again he'd forgotten he had company, Matilda's presence was so thick in the air.

"That will do, for now, thank you," he said, after which the tailor bowed, gathered his tools, and swept from the room.

Celeste, understanding a royal request for privacy when she heard one, quickly followed and shut the door.

Matilda, naturally, had no clue what had just happened. Or didn't imagine his dismissal included her.

He watched in the reflection as she hopped off the chair and padded his way. Her feet bare, as usual, her eyes warm as she slipped in behind him and brought her hands to the collar of his shirt, uncurling it and laying it flat. Only rather than the deft movements of the tailor, hers were slow, soothing, as she smoothed out the creases.

"That's been driving me crazy this whole time."

"Has it now," he asked.

Gaze captured by the slow movements of her fingers in the mirror, he lifted his eyes to hers. The hold of her gaze jerking something loose inside him, prying open some ancient lockbox that had been holding the gentler, softer, warmer feelings that she alone had on a string.

But then her hands slipped away, and she moved to lean against the edge of the mirror. "I think we should do this."

He raised an eyebrow.

And she laughed, not pretending to misunderstand.

"Do something useful, *tomorrow*. I could be in charge of passing you important papers. Or hold your crown when it gets too heavy."

"I was thinking of leaving the crown behind," he said, "what with a possible visit to a fishery, or the government subcommittee on road upgrades, but after your fine offer, I might reconsider."

She grinned and the lockbox inside of him flew open with a flourish, and feelings whipped about inside of him too quickly to catch.

He waited for the *carefully, carefully* to whisper inside his head, but he got nothing.

"Is that a yes?" she asked.

"It's a yes."

She leaped in the air, air punch and all, before telling a story about the one time she'd had a dress tailor-made, for some racing event her parents hosted each year.

And Henri let her voice wash over him as he imagined Andre in the corner, laughing at how quickly he'd capitulated.

Matilda stood by Celeste's side, mirroring her low-key movements as they followed Henri down a reception line of nurses and staff at a local children's hospital.

Celeste, taking the "shadow Celeste" mission literally, had had a half dozen skirt suits and low heels similar to her own sent to Matilda's room that morning. After which, Matilda had decided she might as well go full method—wrangling her hair into a slick low bun and practicing her "capable" face.

She'd been wondering if this was how a princess of Chaleur might be expected to dress— neat, inoffensive, inert—when Henri had jogged down the front steps toward the waiting car, looking strained and tunnel-visioned. Then, having spotted her beside Celeste, he'd done the most delicious double take.

"Matilda?" he'd said. "You look…"

She held out her arms and twirled a little. "Told you I could hide in plain sight."

Henri shook his head and muttered something

in French. She wasn't sure if it was a good mutter, or if he was regretting his decision. For he was in supreme prince mode; fast-moving, fast talking, no smiles, dead serious, the way he'd been on the street that first day.

Making her wonder if his disinclination in regard to public appearances had less to do with time management than he claimed, and more to do with an actual disinclination toward public events.

But then Boris ushered Celeste and Matilda into the back seat of his car, while Henri went with Lars. After which a cavalcade of cars filled with extra security followed, careening down the mountain into town. Everyone a little giddy, as if they had all been hankering for such a day to arrive.

By the time they hit their third event of the day—the visit to a children's hospital—Matilda's feet were starting to pinch, and she could see the curls that had sprung from her bun. Working the land was physically demanding, but the smiling, listening, asking pertinent questions, keeping track of the logistics of cars and staff, names, all while trying to appear as fresh as a daisy was draining in a whole other way.

Not that you'd know it, watching Henri. For whatever stress he'd brought with him into the car that morning, he'd left there.

Around the people, *his* people, he was attentive and generous. They glowed under his gentle charisma, gushed as he shook hands, cooed as he crouched down to chat with kids in wheelchairs and listened to stories the nurses told.

When she'd passed a group of said nurses earlier, they'd pulled her aside, asking what he was like in "real life." She'd paused barely a second before leaning in, telling them how hard he worked, how much he cared for the country, till they looked at him like he was Superman in a suit.

And what had started out as a chance to see more of his country, ended up bittersweet. For it only nailed down how suited he was to the role. If he'd followed her, as she'd begged in the note she'd left him, he'd have missed this chance, and these people would have missed out on him.

Then Celeste cleared her throat to signal to all that it was time to move on, and Henri waved down the line to those he'd not been able to meet, had a quick chat to the administrator and then they were back in the car, on their way home.

No, not *home*. Prince Henri's *château*.

They'd fallen into whichever cars had come first—Celeste in the front seat, beside Boris, who was driving, Matilda in the back with Henri, who filled the space with his long legs, and some unexpectedly dark energy, considering how wonderful he'd been all day.

When he ran a hand over his face, leaving his

matinee idol hair slightly mussed, the furrows in his brow etched in place, she knew something wasn't right.

"Well," she said brightly, the need to play happy-maker surging inside of her. "That last one was my favourite."

His hand dropped to the seat between them as he turned her way. His gaze hard. Apparently broody was a serious kink of hers, as she felt instantly twitchy all over.

"No?" she checked. "Not yours?"

His voice a little raw, as he'd been talking all day, Henri said, "The administrator asserts their funding is about to be cut. Budget constraints put in place by the previous reign."

"The previous reign being your father?"

A muscle ticked in his jaw.

Celeste shifted in the front seat, and a moment later a soundproof barrier slowly lifted into place, cutting the front from the back.

Their body warmth soon intermingled in the tight space. And when Matilda turned on the seat to face Henri, her knee knocked against his, the slide of bare skin against the wool of his pants sending shards of static up and down her body.

"Is it something you can change?" she asked. "Is that something you are able to do?"

He lifted a hand to the back of his neck and gripped it hard, and for a moment she thought he might not answer. That he might be so used to having to shoulder the load alone that he wouldn't let her in.

Till he rumbled, "Budgets are like big ships, slow and cumbersome to turn around."

"But you will try." It was a statement, not a question.

His gaze shifted to hers, his mouth quirking even as his eyes remained dark. "I have pushed parliament's patience rather a lot, especially the past few weeks. But yes, I will try."

"Then I have every faith you'll make it happen."

"I wish I had your belief."

Was it possible Henri did not see himself as the born leader that he so clearly was? She leaned in, her hand landing on his knee. Partly to get his attention and partly to stop her shoulder from bumping the seat in front.

"Henri, did you not see the faces of those you've spent time with today. They adore you. More than that, they trust you."

"They adored my uncle, but they did not know him."

A glimmer of an old conversation came back to her. "Andre said something similar to me once— that your uncle had been beloved by everyone outside of the castle walls. Meaning he hadn't been within?"

The darkness in his eyes only deepened. "He was a proud man who did not take failure well. Leading to a grave mismanagement of resources." Henri's gaze, usually so rich and warm, seemed to recede until he might as well have been behind a pane of glass. "After he was gone, the people then mistook my father's relative charm for a breath of fresh air, rather than seeing him as the crook that he was. Their continued faith in the royal house is not well-placed."

Oh, Henri. Matilda wasn't sure what to say—if she kept gushing, it might come across as insincere. Or worse, look like she was fast developing a crush on her ex-lover-slash-possible-husband who had once let her down so badly she wasn't sure she'd ever quite recovered.

Lucky for her, Henri got in first.

"Which brings me to something that has been weighing on me."

"Okay. Bring it."

"I know we said no promises, no plans—"

"You said that," Matilda reminded him gently. "I'd already planned out at least a dozen different eventualities long before I arrived here."

"Fair," he said, the darkness easing, thank goodness. "Now that I've had time to adjust, there is something that needs to be made clear. If news comes through that the marriage is valid, I will not lie to my people. And I will not put them through the farce of a royal marriage only for it to 'fall apart' a year later. You have enough insight now, I gather, into my family so that you might understand why."

She had some, but she had the feeling it was only the tip of the iceberg.

"So, what you are saying is, if Andre suddenly appears waving a marriage license, we stay the course?"

"Or," Henri offered softly, "we begin divorce proceedings immediately."

Matilda swallowed against the sudden lump in her throat. "Won't *that* be scandalous?"

"Perhaps. But it would be the truth."

For all that every eventuality felt fraught, some now more than others, Matilda's hand squeezed his knee. In support. And to show him that she understood, that she was on his side. Because she had the feeling, that, though he was a fundamentally amazing human, he'd had little of that in his life.

His gaze dropped to her touch. Staying for a few long hot beats, before his hand lifted to cover hers. His fingers curled around her fingers, tangling them. He breathed out hard, as if holding her allowed him to let something go.

"Matilda?" Henri asked, as she must have made some kind of noise. A purr. Or a moan. Good gods, did she have no survival instincts at all?

She gathered herself quick smart and changed the subject, "Do you think we got away with it? Did anyone notice the highly adequate new assistant in your midst?"

Henri's gaze roved over her face, her hair with

its fuzzy curls, then kept on moving, all the way down to her feet, now bare, as she'd nudged off her shoes the moment she'd had the chance.

When his gaze swept back to hers, right as his thumb ran over the back of her hand, finding a magical pressure point, she sucked in a breath.

"If they did not notice you, Matilda, they were looking the wrong way."

At which point he lifted their joined hands to his mouth, placing a kiss to her knuckles, before letting their joined hands drop back to his knee.

And they sat that way for the rest of the drive to Chaleur Castle. Henri now far more at ease.

Meanwhile, Matilda's heart bucked with every bump in the road, her mind busy spinning castles in the sky.

"I hear the hospital visit was a big success," said Andre as he moseyed into Henri's office late that night.

Henri tossed a folder to his desk and ran both hands over his eyes. "That so?"

"Celeste wrote a gushing report." Andre waved his phone. "The press had nothing but good to say. The patients. The staff. All enamoured."

"The funding—"

"I know. I heard. The fact that you were there, on the ground, to hear about it means you can do something about it."

Henri had no comeback there.

"So what's next? I'd suggest a casual stop by the local farmers' market, a night at the National Opera, check in with Summer Festival—"

"I have too much to catch up on here."

"You'll always have too much to catch up on here, unless you learn to delegate. Celeste and I can help you source excellent people to help us bear the brunt of your martyrdom."

It was nothing he hadn't heard before, only he'd made the choice to do the work himself so that there was no chance of misdeed, or misappropriation. Only now Henri actually considered it.

For the venture had been a success, on multiple levels.

Then there were the moments Matilda had broken out of "shadow mode." Chatting and laughing with a couple of nurses, about him he had been sure. Playing one-handed patty-cake with kids in casts in the orthopaedic wing.

While he felt like a spotlight was burning down on him anytime he had to play Prince Henri in public, Matilda was a natural.

"Matilda enjoyed it too."

Andre's expression was neutral, which for Andre said everything.

"Am I being too careful? Keeping her locked up here feels beastly. As if soon townsfolk with pitchforks might come at me."

"Not if the townsfolk know you better." The man was a dog with a bone. "Look, if you are concerned that someone might notice you are spending time with someone of the female persuasion, who freaking cares."

"I do."

Andre bowed. "Then might I suggest you try to rein in your sparkle when she is near."

"My what?"

"Your *sparkle*." Andre batted his lashes. "It's really quite adorable."

Henri swore beneath his breath, before coughing out a laugh. "You've been watching too much *Twilight*."

Andre gasped. "There is no such thing as too much *Twilight*."

And somehow, after that, Henri agreed to trial more public outings. For no matter how the future unfurled, right now he had a job to do. And being around the people was the best way for him to get to know them. What they wanted, what they needed, not what he assumed would make their lives easier.

"We need more people in your retinue," said Andre, seeing his chance to bolster their staff, "who can sweep in and take notes and talk to people and gather the information in your wake."

Henri didn't demur, as the more people in the entourage the less likely Matilda's continued presence would stand out.

One afternoon was spent perusing sweet shops in a local village, famous for their hard candies.

Another was spent donating books to a local library. A third was spent in a private viewing with a local glassblower, who gifted Matilda a glossy green horse that fit into her palm.

"I shall name him Peridot!" she had declared, as apparently all the horses back at Garrison Downs were named after gemstones. The details of her life building a rich picture of who she was and where she'd come from. Every addition sliding beneath his skin, like an itch, a glimmer in his veins.

Not a *sparkle*, as Andre had so delightfully put it.

But close.

Matilda woke up feeling frisky.

The little trips they had been taking in the townships near the château had been delightful. She'd picked up gifts—the glass horse from a local glassblower would go to Rose, a small painting of the château to Eve in the hopes it might call to the sweet romantic side she'd harboured as a kid, and she'd found some charms for Ana who, in the days after the will reading, had quietly admitted that she'd love to one day give up accountancy to concentrate on her fledgling jewellery design business.

And in her downtime she'd drafted three more chapters of her book and begun work on a backlog of letters her old professor had asked her to take a first sweep on authenticating when she had the time.

I could get used to this, she'd thought, and then something had clutched at her chest. *No promises, no plans.*

Heading down to breakfast, she found the dining room empty, a jar of Vegemite now on the breakfast buffet.

Henri, she thought, a fresh wave of warmth swarming through her, making her feel as if fireflies fluttered under her skin. And while she usually waited till lunchtime to give in to the urge to see him, her feet took her to his office. Promising herself she'd thank him for the Vegemite, then leave him be.

She found him there, in the dark, the curtains still closed up from the night before. He sat not behind his desk but in a chair, finger running over his mouth, forehead creases creasing like never before.

And he stared hard at an envelope he held in his hand.

She'd seen enough fancy letters in her time to pick up on its import—heavy, expensive paper, several pages thick, official looking, with a thick red wax seal.

"Henri?" she said, taking a step or two his way.

He looked up, his gaze unreachable. Impenetrable. *Regal.* As if with a wave of his hand he might banish her.

But the moment he saw her, his gaze cleared. And it was really hard not to read things into that. Not to let it slide beneath her skin and stay there.

"What you got there?" she asked, motioning to the envelope.

Henri's gaze returned to the envelope, and the storm clouds were back.

Having grown up surrounded by strong silent men, she was not fazed. Moving around his chair, she leaned down to ask. "Is it…an electricity bill? A place this size, it must be exorbitant."

Henri huffed out a deep breath. "Electricity, water, they are all state owned. Free for all citizens."

"Well, that's nice." She folded her arms along the back of the chair. "So, if it's not a bill, I'm thinking…jury duty?"

"I am exempt."

"Oh, to be a prince! If it's not a bill, and it's not jury duty—"

"Parliament have been polling the constituency as to the viability of holding a referendum as to whether or not the royal house of Raphael-Rossetti remains a valid means to oversee the political state of Chaleur."

Matilda's hands lifted off the back of the chair as if burned. She moved to stand in front of Henri, arms crossed. "Have they not *met* you? Have they not seen how hard you work? Have they not seen how the people react when you spend time with them? How deeply you listen and care?"

Henri's gaze had lifted to hers, his eyes moving over her face as she ranted. Which only made her rant more.

"How could they do such a thing—"

"Because I asked them to."

"What?" she whispered. Then, "You want to dismantle the monarchy from within?"

He looked to the envelope again, before tossing it to the lamp table at his side. Then he sat forward, elbows on knees, and ran his hands over his face.

Matilda found the nearest empty chair and dragged it so that she was sitting in front of him. Close enough their knees nearly touched. Close enough he'd have to climb over her to escape.

"Talk to me."

She thought he might brush her off. Go all stoic and strong. But when his gaze landed on hers, he told her his story.

"When it became clear that my uncle, Prince Augustus, was unable to have an heir, he made it his mission to groom the next generation of Raphael-Rossettis into an army of impeccable princes and princesses. We were indoctrinated in diplomacy, behaviour, proper language. Drilled in the fact that we were different, better, and must hold ourselves apart. Forced to repeat affirmations as to our God-given right to rule, hundreds of times, every day. For years. And it was made clear that our thoughts, our lives, our futures were not our own. That they belonged to Chaleur."

Matilda's hand was at her mouth, pressed to her lips as she tried to imagine the childhood Henri was describing.

"There were dozens of us, Andre included, though the numbers dissipated when it became clear how obsessed he had become. Until it was just me."

"Your parents?" she asked.

"My mother was long gone, my father happy to have me out of his hair. That summer—*our* summer—I had negotiated three months away, a final burst of freedom before returning to the fold. But I had no intention of returning. Especially after Vienna."

His gaze found hers. And their entire relationship existed in that look.

Their connection instant. Their relationship, hot and fast and fierce. Her naivete trusted life could be that way forever. While he'd been trying to live a lifetime in a single summer.

"My uncle abdicated the day summer ended. Fleeing to Brazil, having made horrifically damaging financial and political decisions, only to die there months later. And so I returned, as he'd known I would. Waiting in the wings until my turn came."

Oh, Henri.

"I wouldn't wish that on anyone, much less a child. But I'm not sure that burning down his house will fix anything."

She'd had that urge herself in the days after her father's will reading as she'd flipped from sorrow, to fear, to anger. Screw him and the fortune he'd built. Let it fall apart. Only time, and love for her sisters, had eased it to a dull pain.

Henri looked away from her then, out the window or into the past, she couldn't be sure. "It's not that. Or not only that. In centuries past, it made sense to have the protection of a royal family who represented a country's history, its interests, its cultural identity. But now? It's too much power, and too much responsibility for one man."

All that frisky energy from earlier compacted into something sharper, more focused. Matilda shuffled to perch on the edge of her chair, then reached out and took Henri's hand.

His gaze dropped to the contact. Staring at their joined hands as he slipped his more fully into hers.

"Henri, what's in the envelope?"

"I imagine it will be the results of the poll."

"You haven't looked?"

He shook his head.

"Would you like me to do the honours? I promise, if the results are dim, I won't like you any less."

Henri laughed, though it was more of a moan. Used to the low light now, she saw, when his gaze lifted to hers, a question shift mercurially across his eyes.

How much do you like me now?

But then he reached for the envelope and handed it to her.

She took back her hand and ran her fingers over the paper. She usually saw such beautiful workmanship decades, or even centuries, after its import had faded. This was living history.

Yet, she wished she had a fire going nearby so she could toss it in the flames. If a single person had made a snide comment about this man, she'd wish boils upon their nether regions.

"Before what a bunch of strangers have to say becomes a part of how you see yourself forevermore, I need you to hear me." She looked up to find Henri looking deep into her eyes. "I think you might be a masochist."

At that he laughed, then leaned back into the chair. "How do you come to that conclusion?"

She waved a hand at him. "You are determined to make up for the mistakes of your uncle, your father, your brother, and probably another dozen ancestors who committed absolute horrors in the name of God and country. When all you have to do to improve this place is be you. The fact that you worry that you can't do the job justice is *exactly* why you will." Then, "And lastly, while I don't know all that many princes, I'd bet everything I have that you are top-tier."

"Is that so?"

Henri's gaze swept over her then, his nostrils flaring, his eyes hot. As if… Well, as if he'd like nothing more than to drag her onto his lap and kiss her. And she knew in that moment that if he did so, she'd let him.

But this had to come first.

Praying that the people of Chaleur had the slightest clue how lucky they were, she tore open the envelope without ceremony and speed-read pages of statistics, pie graphs, and explanatory prose.

It didn't take long to note that the patterns were clear.

"I knew I liked this country of yours, Henri." Her smile was so wide her cheeks ached. "Turns out they are *overwhelmingly* in favour of things remaining just as they are. And don't go thinking its due to some rose-coloured vision of the past or misplaced respect for your forebears. It's all you."

She handed over the papers.

Watching impatiently for Henri to say *huzzah*, as he read over the poll data, instead she watched as he read, and read, and read. Appearing to be completely and utterly in shock.

After a good while, he let the papers drop and lifted his eyes back to hers. "Thank you."

"For what? Anyone can open an envelope."

"Not with quite as much panache." One corner of his mouth hooked into a half smile and she was glad to be sitting down. For she felt like a champagne bottle uncorked, the fizz no longer in her control.

Matilda swallowed, some latent thread of self-protection warning her that the longer she remained, the more these feelings would wind about her heart like the ivy covering the walls of his castle.

"Do you have a minute?" he asked, breaking into her mild but important panic.

"I have all the minutes," she said, grinning like a fool.

"I'd like to show you something."

"Great!" she said, while frantically wondering how one might best hack metaphorical ivy clear. Before it was too late.

CHAPTER SIX

HENRI STOOD IN the doorway to his family's famous library—two stories high, gloriously appointed, filled with books that had been lost to other countries in coups and revolutions, kept safe here due to the longevity his family had ensured—and watched as Matilda made her way around the room.

Despite knowing how much she would love it, he'd avoided bringing her here, as this was the room in which his uncle's "lessons" had taken place.

He waited for the ghosts of his uncle's voice, the snap of leather across his knuckles. Only when he focused on Matilda, humming happily as her fingers trailed over spines of books, as she stopped and looked at framed family letters, copies of important speeches, the original plans for the château, he managed to keep the rest at bay.

There would be no referendum.

Meaning that this was where he would remain. Through all his days. Serving the people of Chaleur. When he'd imagined this possible outcome, he was certain he'd feel bereft. Lost to history before he'd even lived it. But for some reason that feeling had yet to eventuate.

Matilda, he thought. It was entirely due to Matilda. Not only her impassioned speech before she'd opened the envelope but the way she'd nudged him back out into the world again. As if she'd been sent to him, at the exact right moment he'd needed her obstreperous positivity most.

"Henri," she said, as she turned to him, her expression saying *I can't believe you were hiding this from me.*

"I had a feeling you'd like this room."

"I feel like Elizabeth Bennett when she first saw Pemberley." Then, "Do you remember the book of letters and poetry I bought you, the one with the blue cover?"

Of course he remembered.

"Is it here somewhere?"

"It's…it's been a while since I've seen it." He moved into the room. "As I remember it, you particularly liked the Emerson."

Liked him reading it to her in bed, her limbs twisted about his, her head on his chest.

She watched him as he neared, her gaze glinting, as if he knew *exactly* what she was remembering. *"'Thou art to me a delicious torment,'"* she quoted. "Heady stuff."

While the next line echoed in Henri's head: *Thine ever, or never.*

"Come here," he said, moving to the bookshelves in the corner.

And watched as she swallowed. Her cheeks warming. Her breaths coming a little harder and faster.

He ran his finger under a particular shelf. Felt the slight nub, pressed it, and a secret door popped free.

Matilda let out a delighted laugh, which was swallowed by a soft gasp when she entered the hidden room—temperature controlled with a soft light around the edges of the floor that warmed to a soft glow as they entered.

In the centre of the tight space stood a glass stand containing a single piece of paper.

"That," said Henri, his voice low, reverent, "is the letter assuring recognition of our independent sovereignty from France by Louis XIII in 1642. Bar a short stretch in the early eighteen hundreds, during the French Revolution, Chaleur has been under the protection of the Raphael-Rossetti family ever since."

And it looked as if it would remain that way at least a while longer.

Matilda leaned closer, eyes drinking in the curve of the paper, the sweep of the signature with its slight splatter of ink at the end, the royal seal. "Henri," she whispered. "This is the real deal."

"Are you a letter *writer* still?" She'd written every night when he'd known her. Pages of descriptive joyful prose.

She lifted her eyes to his. They were dark in the low light. Gleaming. "It's been a while."

"Why?" he asked, moving around the case to look over her shoulder at the document. And so he could be closer to her. For while he'd been fighting it this entire time, and now a great weight had lifted off his shoulders, he couldn't remember why.

"No one to write letters to, I guess."

Her shoulders hitched, and he caught a waft of her scent. Sweet green apple, summer sunshine, and something earthier that further loosened the knots inside of him.

"You were writing to your mother," he said, the memory coming full circle.

Her eyes closed a moment before she blinked them open. "It was kind of our thing."

"How so?"

"It started when I went to boarding school—common for kids from farming families. Rose hated it and lasted a year before convincing our parents to let her head home and finish via correspondence. I'm not sure it was right for Eve either. She was such a sweetie, kind of shy, romantic, but she changed during those years. While I was so excited to *be* somewhere new. Every week my mother would send me a new book—history or travel or biography—with a handwritten letter tucked into the first page, telling a tale of how it had moved her."

She let her finger touch the corner of the glass, as if the tactile connection made it more real. "Letters became a fascination. Letters between soldiers at war and their sweethearts. Between authors and their siblings. Between poets and their muses. The intimate stories behind the public facade."

She took a breath and turned to face him. Close enough that even in the low light he could clock the myriad blues in her bright eyes.

"I'd been chasing such a letter when I was in Vienna. I so wanted to tell you all about it that night, but with Andre's rules stuck in my head I was terrified I'd lose access to...well, to you."

The room seemed to shrink around him. Then her mouth kicked up at one corner and the urge to touch the spot with his thumb, to tug at her bottom lip, to kiss her there, to know if she tasted as she once had, was like a whirlpool dragging him under.

"Tell me now," he said.

"Well, the owner of the letter was an old lady who spoke very little English. I had to drink copious amounts of very strange tea to earn her trust. Then I had to convince her to send her most treasured possession to the other side of the world for authentication."

"Did you, convince her?"

"I did. People find it very hard to say no to me."

Henri smiled. And time seemed to beat between them then, or perhaps that was just him. The whump of his blood as it rocketed around his body. Reaching places he'd long since believe atrophied. Lost when he'd lost her.

"I've missed this," Henri whispered, the words falling from his mouth, before he even felt the words coming. "I've missed the way I am with you."

Matilda blinked in surprise. Of course she did. For he no longer had the right to say such things. To assume—

"I've missed you too," she said, her voice breaking.

And there it was. The great, churning truth they had been politely dancing around for days. Despite past hurts, despite the fact that they were different people now, the connection they had once shared had been meaningful and bigger than both of them.

Matilda leaned into him then, her fingers lifting to curl into his shirt, her forehead landing against his chest.

And while he felt sure that giving in to the feelings swarming through him was a dangerous game, a beginning with an end built in, it was a battle already lost.

Henri slid his arms around her back, slowly,

relearning the shape of her. Her softness and her strength. When she curved her body into his, he hauled her close and held her there.

"I'm sorry we didn't break the rules sooner," she said. "Didn't tell one another everything. It feels like so much wasted time."

His hand moved to her chin, lifted it gently, held it so that she could not look away. "You have nothing to apologise for. Even if you had told me everything, back then I didn't wish to be known."

Her body trembled against his. Or perhaps it was him, vibrating with the need to touch her, all of her. When her tongue darted out to wet her lips, the urge to chase it with his own was nearly his undoing.

Instead his thumb traced her cheekbone. His fingers moving into her hair. The thick waves spilling over his wrist like warm silk.

Rather than their twin storms colliding, as they once had, the air around them seemed to settle on a whisper of a sigh, as Matilda's hand gripped his shirt tighter and she lifted onto her toes.

As if it was the most natural thing in the world, Henri met her halfway.

When his lips found hers, he felt as if he'd been marking time. Waiting for this moment his entire life. The touch of her mouth tentative yet familiar. The taste sweet and fresh and completely her.

Soft, learning sips soon grew into something slick and loose and achingly lovely. And when her hands crept up his chest, around his neck, so that she could press herself harder against him, a small moan of pleasure rose in the back of her throat.

And it became a slow burn of moving hands, shifting bodies. Slanting mouths and the world beneath him tipping and swaying.

When Matilda's leg wrapped around his, as if she wanted to climb onto him, *into* him, he lifted her into his arms. Carried her till her back hit the wall. His mouth tracing her jaw, her throat. Drinking in her scent—

Then came a whistle and footsteps, then the squeak of shoes on polished wood floor, followed by a familiar voice, saying, "Cousin? Ah."

Andre appeared in the doorway, his expression comically surprised as he said, *"Merde. Je suis désolé,"* before disappearing back into the library proper.

And like a bucket of cold water had been tossed over them both, Henri slowly came back into his own body. To find he had a hand up the back of Matilda's T-shirt, while hers was inside the collar of his, the hem of which had been pulled free of his suit pants.

Her spare hand went to her mouth, whether to hold back a groan or a laugh, he could not be sure.

Slowly they disentangled themselves from one

another. Her hands moving to do up a slipped button of his shirt, his smoothing the back of her top.

"You okay?" he asked.

"Depends what you mean by okay."

Henri moved so he could see her face. The wild wide eyes, the plump moisture of her lips. "We need to go back out there, eventually," he said.

"Or," she said with the insouciant lift of a shoulder, "you could order your cousin to go away. Surely being a sovereign prince has some advantages."

Henri laughed. Then allowed himself a few last moments to imprint how she looked on his memory before he took her by the hand, led her out of the hidden room, and gently shut the door.

Andre was leaning against the back of a couch, his gaze on where their hands were joined. "I'm sorry, am I interrupting something?"

"Not at all," lied Henri.

"It's just… I heard a letter was delivered. With the parliamentary seal."

Matilda, behind him, leaned her forehead against his back a moment before she moved away. "I'll leave you guys to it. Thank you," she said turning to walk backward, facing Henri, "for showing me your special room."

"Is that what they call it these days?" Andre asked.

She shot Andre a look, crossed her eyes at him, then waltzed out the library door.

"The envelope?" Andre reminded him. And Henri, who had tucked it onto his pocket for safe-keeping, passed it over.

And while Andre poured over the data, Henri was left to wonder how far things might have gone if Andre had not found them when he had.

When the referendum was still a possibility, there was a chance he might yet be able to make choices that affected only him. But now that hope was gone.

Everything he did from now on had to be about the crown.

Whether that included Matilda, or excluded her, was still to be seen.

Hours later, having heard nothing from Henri since she'd left the library, Matilda paced her suite, the phone ringing and ringing and ringing as per usual when she tried to call Eve.

Because she *really* needed to talk to someone who was Team Matilda. A big sister who had been obsessed with romance novels growing up seemed just the ticket.

Which was why, rather than hanging up, as she usually did, she left a sassy message. "Hey, Evie, this is Matilda. Your sister. Remember me? Just calling to let you know I just kissed a prince. Who might be my husband. And, since that's just the kind of thing you'd once upon a time have eaten up with a spoon, I thought maybe you could talk me down from the ledge I'm currently dancing on."

She pressed finger and thumb to her temples.

"Or not. Whatever. Anyway, if you actually listen to this message, don't tell Rose. And get off your high horse and call Ana. She's sweet and none of this is her fault. And—"

The phone beeped when she ran out of time. She tossed her phone on the bed, then followed, landing on her front like a starfish.

What had she been thinking?

Things had been going nicely with Henri. They'd been learning about one another, communicating well, being supportive. Keeping things cool and measured—the opposite of whirlwind.

Then she'd grabbed him by the shirt and kissed him.

But, oh, what a kiss. Like the reins had snapped, and all the feelings and memories and longing they'd been holding back had been set free.

Yes, they'd kissed before. A lot. But they'd been so young then, swept up in the drama and responsibility-free disconnect of a holiday romance.

Now, with context and experience and maturity at their backs, *new* feelings were at play. Respect and fascination, comfort and a sense of safe harbor. Feelings that ran wide and deep.

Which might have been a nice thing, a lovely thing, if there wasn't so much at stake.

She shimmied up the bed, found her phone and texted Rose. Needing a solid reminder of just what that thing was.

Rose: Hey! What's up?

Matilda: What's up with you?

Rose: Johnno had a fall, broke his wrist. Sally stood on a rusty nail so had to head into the Marni clinic for a tetanus booster. River went missing for half a day before we found him locked in the coat closet.

Matilda: So, nothing out of the ordinary.

Matilda rolled onto her back, holding her phone above her, feeling a comforting stab of guilt at not being there. Not that she'd ever been much good at mustering, or patching up busted staff, or remembering to shut gates. But she was a queen when it came to keeping up morale.

Matilda: Need me to come home?

Coward.

Rose: We are fine here without you!

Matilda: Well, that's nice to hear.

Rose: We miss you terribly, of course. River especially.

Matilda: He would.

Matilda: He's a good dog.

Matilda: Unlike the rest of you.

Rode: *laughing emoji*

Rose: Stop fretting. This is my vision board, not yours.

Matilda's face felt unusually warm as she typed.

Matilda: Meaning?

Rose: Helping to run a cattle station isn't what you really want to do with your life.

Matilda: Says who.

Rose: Anyone who's ever met you.

Rose: Gotta go. Talk soon. xxx

Matilda stared at the messages, reading over them again. Then she sat up, feeling as if she'd been smacked across the back of the head. Twice.

Sure, she'd stayed home not because being a farmer was her dream and not because she wanted to be there more than anywhere else, and… What was the point she was trying to make again?

Feeling tetchier now than she had *before* she'd contacted her sisters, Matilda pushed herself off the bed and went to her desk. Tried to write, but couldn't see the words on the screen. Tried to check her emails, but couldn't concentrate.

And in the end found herself back outside Henri's office.

Pacing to the door, then walking away. Then pacing back to the door again, where she rapped three times and entered.

He sat behind his desk, looking harried. His gaze was on his monitor as he typed something, his brow furrows deep and ingrained.

"Sit," he said, "I'll be a minute."

Matilda perched on the chair across from his desk feeling like she was back in the principal's office—having to explain herself inciting a strike unless an excursion to a museum she wanted to visit was included in the curriculum. Generally causing havoc in the name of trying to get whatever it was she wanted.

Rose's words came back to her: *Helping run a cattle station isn't what you want to do with your life.*

Henri chose *that* moment to stop stewing and sit back and say, "Matilda—"

This time she got in first. "We kissed," she blurted.

A beat slunk by before he sat forward, steepling his hands on his desk. "I noticed."

Matilda curled her feet up onto the chair in the hopes of holding in the sensations rocketing through her. "Kissing wasn't part of the deal."

"As far as I remember we had no deal bar—"

"No promises, no plans." *Right.* "So kissing is okay then?"

Something in the set of his shoulders, the directness of his gaze, made her sure he was about to enact a royal decree, negating all chance of further action between them. Until he breathed, deeply, his nostrils flaring as if he'd caught her scent on the air. And she wondered if he was only just holding himself together too.

"I think creating a set of rules that we must arbitrarily follow has not worked out so well for us in the past. Trusting that as adults we can communicate, consider, and make decisions on the fly seems sensible."

"Sensible," she repeated.

When all she could think was that it hadn't only been her mother's passing that had kept her at Garrison Downs. The ease with which Henri had cut her off had meant she no longer trusted her gut instinct. Which until then had been her superpower. Her driving force.

"If you agree," she said, choosing her words

carefully, "that following a set of arbitrary rules has not worked out so well for us in the past, why was I the one who was punished for breaking them?"

Henri baulked. "I'm not sure what you mean."

"My note, of course."

She was doing this now? Yes, yes, she was. For it was all tangled up in the moment in her life where everything had shifted. The spanner jarred in the mechanism of her life, all her dreams coming to a grinding halt. Where she'd lost more than her mother—she'd lost herself.

Henri's jaw ticked. "I'm not sure how that relates—"

"The rules, Andre's rules. We stuck to them, faithfully, the entire time. Until I wrote that note. And then…" She swallowed, unprepared for the emotions it would reignite. "Then nothing. Silence. As if we had never been."

Henri blinked. And blinked again. "You were the one who left, Matilda."

"But the note!"

Henri ran his hands over his face, then looked at her as if she'd started speaking another language. "I did what I had done each day that week. Woke early, kissed your sleeping forehead. Made my side of the bed, even while knowing yours would stay rumpled. Took the speedboat into town to go for a run, pick up coffee, breakfast, the paper, provisions. I came back just before lunch to find a torn-off scrap of paper on my pillow stating you were sorry and you had to leave. And I never heard from you again."

Matilda opened her mouth to argue, before she realised there was a huge disconnect. "I couldn't contact you, Henri. I had no way. Which is why I left all my details. On the note."

Something in the way Henri stilled, his aura cooling before fading away entirely, had Matilda's instincts crackling. Like they were finally, *finally* sputtering back to life.

"Matilda," Henri said, his words slow and careful. "There were no details on the note. All it said was *I am sorry. I had to go.*"

She waited for the rest. But it was clear he was done.

"I... Yes, that's how it began. Followed by the news that Rose had called, and my mother was in a coma. I scrawled down my phone number, my address, my email." She swallowed. "And I asked if you would follow me, when you could. I knew I'd need you during what was to come."

Henri sat back, his hand tight on the back of his neck. "There was only one note."

"Only one."

"The one I found on your pillow."

"I never put it on my pillow..."

The trauma of that event meant Matilda remembered only patches of that morning, but those she did she remembered with aching clarity.

Her phone buzzing and buzzing, waking her from a dream. Rousing her far earlier than she preferred, and finding a dozen messages from Rose.

"Henry?" she'd called. "Henry!" Then, realising Henry would have only just headed off, she'd gone looking for Andre and found him sitting on the bow, reading a book.

Andre had looked up. Stood up. "Matilda, what is wrong? Are you hurt?"

"It's my mother. I have to get home."

"Of course." Andre had pulled out a phone and begun speaking in fast French. She'd recognised some of it—plane, Australia, and her name. He rang off with a clipped *"Merci."* Then said, "My agent is organising a flight now."

"Thank you. But what about Henry—"

"You need to go, correct?"

She'd nodded.

"You pack. I will organise transport to get you to the airport. Diplomatic channels will get you on a plane within the hour." Hand to his heart, he'd said, "I will look after Henry."

And so, in a tunnel of panic and fear, she'd tossed her gear into her suitcase. Made sure she had her phone, passport etc. Then she'd ripped a page of notepaper from a notepad with the name of the charter company atop, and written:

I'm so sorry. I have to go. My sister mes-saged. My mum is really sick.

After an infinitesimal pause, she'd written her name, address, email, and phone number. Signing off with *Please come, if you can. I love you. M*

Back in Henri's office, her blood rushed fast behind her ears.

"I didn't leave the note on the pillow, Henri. I gave it to Andre."

Henri found Andre in the billiard room, lining up a small six. "I need to talk to you. Now."

"I have no news as yet," said Andre, rolling his shoulder and hunching over the cue. "Though I am on it. Every breath I take."

Henry leaned over and picked up the six. "I just spoke with Matilda. About the note she left me the day she left."

Andre let the cue slacken, then stood tall. "You read it. Several thousand times over the next weeks."

"She claims it was longer. Conveying how I might get in touch with her. And that she gave it to you." Henri looked to his cousin. Search-ing for tells.

There, the quick sniff that showed he was damn well lying.

He tossed the ball back onto the table and turned away, his hand tight to the back of his neck.

A few breaths later Andre spoke again. "I did what I felt I had to do."

Years spent learning how to curb his emotions was the only thing keeping Henri from grabbing the cue and snapping it in half.

"Why?" he gritted out, his voice raw.

"You think Boris and Lars are your only bodyguards, cousin? I've been doing the job since I was eight years old."

"What does that even *mean*?" Henri threw both arms to the side, then paced down the opposite length of the table. Better that than expel the energy coursing through him by decking the man.

"Augustus was not the only one who saw your potential. Who hoped that you might one day make it to the throne."

Henri ran a hand over his face and stared at his cousin. Feeling as if he was seeing him for the first time.

Andre took a step his way, before something in Henri's bearing pulled him up short. He held out placating hands instead. "When you were determined to make that trip, to have your…Summer of Freedom, I left a very cushy gig running my nice café slash bar, right on the beach, so that I might stick to you like glue. I created the Privacy Pact, acting like a goddamn Doberman, curating our group with people I hoped I could trust not to give you away. People on whom I had enough dirt it was worth their while to stay quiet."

"Why?" Henri asked. Which felt like the least of all the questions building inside of him.

Andre threw his arms in the air. "In case you did something stupid, something self-destructive that might follow you forever and make it impossible for you to trust that you could do this job." Andre stared at Henri. Waiting for the penny to drop.

"Say it," Henri growled.

"You did it anyway. You married Matilda."

"She was not some mode of self-destruction. She was—"

"What?" Andre asked, his voice careful, his tone patient. As if now that he'd admitted to what he'd done, putting their long, trusted relationship at risk, he had no qualms in saying his piece if it knocked something loose inside Henri.

But Henri did not wish to be knocked. Did not wish to feel loose. Or out of control. It was enough for the red mist to begin to clear.

"So you are admitting you read the note, altered it, and knew how to get in contact with her, all these years."

Andre's hands lifted to his hips and he shook his head. "I'm telling you, cousin, I knew who she was within an hour of you first meeting her."

Henri took a step back, wasted years roiling like a stormy sea inside of him. "You knew who she was, and you never told me."

"You never asked."

Henri looked to Andre in disbelief. "Are you kidding me, right now?"

But Andre was not to be cowed. "You were a prince of Chaleur. You had access to all the same contacts I did. And you were the favourite of Augustus, a man who clearly believed the world owed him whatever he desired. If you wanted to find her, you only had to ask."

It wasn't true. He was so smitten with her, he'd have followed her to the ends of the earth, if he'd had the slightest chance. Wouldn't he?

"Just as you could also have found out if the marriage was valid, years ago. Hell, you could have had it annulled."

"No," said Henri, remembering the wedding night, and the days after, in such detail it made his body temperature kick up a notch. "I could not."

Andre crossed his arms. "Never thought I'd see the day I know more about Chaleurian law than you. Turns out, unsurprisingly, a particularly randy forebear created a law allowing for royalty to have a marriage annulled anytime it suited. If you wish it, it can be done."

Henri ran a hand over his face and laughed. There was no humour in it. In fact, he rather felt like kicking something. Andre would do nicely.

Until Andre said, "You can't do it though, can you. And you know why? You are a romantic, cousin. And a martyr. A doomed love affair has suited you and the image you have of yourself far more than a holiday fling ever could. And she was nineteen, Henri, you not much older. The lives of thousands of people were about to turn on what you did next. *My* people."

Andre's words hit like a sling of arrows. Every one of them uncomfortable, painful even. Possibly because they were true. If he'd followed, if he'd been with Matilda when Augustus had abdicated, would he have stayed? Or would he be exactly where he was now?

It did not make Andre's unilateral decision to take it out of his hands forgivable.

"Henri," said Andre, begging him to see sense, "If my choice was so very wrong, and you still want to be with her, marry her. Now. For real."

Henri shook his head. "It's not that simple."

For they'd only just begun to know one another again. And even if their attraction was still there, a living breathing thing, asking her to take on a role he'd fought against his whole life would be the single most selfish thing he could ever do.

But if the decision was out of his hands…

Hands clasped tight behind his back, Henri tilted his chin toward the door. "Go," he said. "Right now. And find me that marriage license."

Andre nodded, with ever so slightly exaggerated deference. And then he was gone.

* * *

Henri strode through the château in search of Matilda.

As if he was back then, on that yacht, he spotted reminders of her everywhere. A pair of sandals by the front door. A coffee cup left on a hall table. She could just as easily be walking a barefoot circle in the rose garden or hanging in the kitchen eating croissant scraps with the cook.

In the end he found her sitting by a window in the downstairs sitting room, her feet curled up onto a chair, a book face down on her knees as she looked pensively down the front drive. Wistfully. Wanting out? Or wanting home?

"Matilda."

She flinched and turned, her expression miserable. As if she too had been contemplating what might have been if Andre had let things run their course.

"Are you okay?" she asked, uncurling from the chair. "You took off like a bat out of hell."

"I'm fine," he said.

She glanced at the hand he held out, swallowed, then padded the final few feet to take it in hers.

Better than fine, he thought, tugging her a little closer. For his focus was sharp, his way clear. "Do you want to get out of here."

"Always," she said with a laugh. He felt like a beast for having kept her cooped up as much as he had. "Is this a Celeste suit-type trek, or are we winging it?"

"No Celeste suit." *Never again.* "I'm thinking something a little different."

"Oh?"

"I've not taken a break in the two years since my coronation. Not once."

"Really?" she said, looking him up and down. "But you seem so chill."

The glint in her eye had him moving in, watching as her chin lifted and her throat worked as the air between them disappeared. "I was thinking... we go south."

"We are about as south as we can go before landing in the Mediterranean."

"Not if we go to Garrison Downs."

Matilda's whole face changed. Shock, then joy, then a flicker of uncertainty, then back to joy. "Are you serious?"

"Deadly."

"But how? Why?"

He lifted a hand to sweep her hair from her cheek, and her bright blue eyes deepened. Darkened. The wish to kiss her again, to sweep her off her feet and into his bed, was potent.

"You've seen mine," he said, his voice rough as his gaze followed the sweep of pink warming her cheeks. "Only fair you show me yours."

Matilda blinked her way out of a haze, and

shook her head. "Are you okay? Is there a chance you've come down with a sudden fever?"

He lifted his gaze back to hers. To that face. Open, trusting. Captivating. "You've come all this way in the hopes of protecting your home. And you're asking for my help to do so. I think it's only fair I see it in person."

Her smile was quick, but quickly chased by concern. For him, or on her own account he could not be sure. All he knew was that he had to do this. He had to know what he'd missed.

"Who will be in charge with you gone?" she asked.

"I will. It's called working remotely."

She looked to the door. "Is Andre okay with this?"

A muscle ticked in his jaw. "Do you want to show me Garrison Downs, or not? Because if I have to invite myself again—"

She shook her head, laughed, then threw herself into his arms. "I want you to come. Please."

As he held her, he thought how every step of his life, *including* what he'd thought had been that single summer of freedom, had been shaped, *reduced*, by some document or other.

A birth certificate, a royal decree, a political poll, a torn note, and now a looming marriage license, all of which decided the path his life would take.

He needed to do this. He needed to know what life might have been like if the choice had been his.

For whether he gave himself up to history, did what others deemed the right thing to do, or went his own way, in the end the choice had always been his.

CHAPTER SEVEN

Garrison Downs,
August

DESPITE THE COMFORT of a private plane, and diplomatic fast-tracking, after twenty-four hours in the air—including a light plane from Adelaide to a local airstrip—then a wild drive through miles of Mars-like Outback terrain that Matilda had *insisted* was part of the experience, Henri was relieved when Matilda slowed at a grand wooden archway, bull horns carved into the arch, heralding the entrance to Garrison Downs.

It was late afternoon, with patchy gum trees sending long shadows over the bumpy driveway, only to finally reveal a sprawling mansion, with wide front verandas, a high gabled roof, and stunning landscaping.

"So, what do you think?" Matilda asked.

"I admit I had pictured a few cattle grazing lazily in a paddock. A wraparound porch. Flies buzzing around a small dam."

Matilda grinned as she pulled the rented four-wheel drive up to the front of the house with a scrape of tyres. "We have all that. Just a million times better."

Henri alighted from the car and stretched his legs, red dust kicking up from the slide of his boot and coating the bottom of his chinos. For all the blinding sunshine, the cold was real. As if everything was bigger here, harder, tougher.

He liked it very much.

A collie jogged around the corner of the house, tongue lolling happily.

Matilda cried, "River! Here, boy!"

The dog bounded to her on old legs, stopping only as she dropped to her knees and pulled him into a tight embrace, her face nuzzling into his neck as she murmured sweet nothings.

When she scrambled back to her feet, the dog came to Henri. He held out a hand for a sniff. "River?"

"River. Was a working dog, now retired. Blossom, Rose's dog, and Lavender will be around somewhere. Come on, let's get your bag inside before the red dust makes havoc of the pretty leather."

"One moment," he said, pulling out his phone to tap out a message to Boris and Lars, who they had dropped at a motel in the nearest town, Marni, much to their protestations. He assured them he'd arrived safe and sound, as if they hadn't already secreted some kind of GPS tracker on his person.

Then, hooking his soft leather bag over his shoulder, he followed Matilda toward the house. Gum trees swished and sang overhead. The caw of a crow broke the heavy silence.

When his gaze dropped to Matilda, who had fallen into step beside him, it was to find her expression hopeful, vulnerable, as if it mattered to her what he thought.

There was also a glimmer of wariness. Which she soon explained, turning to walk backward toward the house, River jogging gently at her side.

"One small thing. My sister Rose, *still* doesn't know about you."

"In what capacity?"

"In any capacity. I rang to let her know we were coming, but Lindy—our housekeeper—answered saying Rose, Aaron—the head stockman—and a handful of the skeleton winter staff are at the Outstation for a few nights. Mobile coverage at the house is top-notch, but there's not much in the way of reception without a satellite phone out there."

She tilted her chin toward the beyond.

"So, she's in for a nice surprise upon her return?"

"Something like that," Matilda said, then turned and jogged up ahead to open the front door.

Once inside, she motioned for him to dump

his bag in a mudroom hidden behind an elegant door, the space filled with gum boots, rain slickers, wide brimmed hats in lieu of woollen winter coats and scarves that would be found in such a room back home.

"Are you too tired for the grand tour?" she asked.

"No," he said, curious gaze taking in wide halls, cream walls, high ceilings, the polished wood floors, and antique furnishings.

But, eyes twinkling, she took his hand again and pulled him back outside. "Not there," she said. "There."

Then tipped her chin toward the acres of dry red landscape beyond.

It was midwinter in this part of the world and yet Henri could feel sweat dripping down his back.

Riding, to him, consisted of weekly lessons in a dressage ring. Polo tournaments in his teens. This was a completely different beast. The saddles were harder, the reins worn in for other hands. The terrain untended, all rocky pastures and tufty hillocks and boulder-filled streams.

Matilda, on the other hand, looked utterly at ease. Her hands loose, her shoulders relaxed, her body moving gracefully as the horse beneath her trotted briskly up unexpected rises and slowed to a lolloping walk any time they hit flat earth.

As if she could feel his eyes on her, she glanced

back. Then with a quick smile, the kind that set off sunbursts behind his eyes, she made a clicking sound and set off at a canter toward a nearby hill.

Henri wished he had a moment to collect himself, lest his chances of ever producing a Raphael-Rossetti heir became moot, but soon his horse, a docile mount named Beryl, followed Matilda's mount with no help from him.

Atop the hill, low sunlight speared shards of pale gold wintry light through a canopy of trees, dappling the leaf-covered floor and creating a kind of dreamscape as Matilda slowly eased her way through, picking out a path.

Cocooned by the shuffle of hooves and soft nasal breaths of the horses, Henri could not have felt further away from the challenges of court. And soon his mind wandered.

An heir. It was a concept he'd refused to entertain, having been one himself and borne the scars of it his whole life. But wasn't that part of why he was here, in this wild, remote, upside-down place? To stretch the possibilities. To think new thoughts. To question everything that had brought him to this moment.

"All okay back there?" Matilda called. "You're terribly quiet."

That's because I'm having an epiphany.

"Just trying to stay upright."

She snorted. "I checked your seat. You're doing just fine."

He readjusted his grip and trotted so that he took a tree to the left while she took it to the right, and soon they were walking side by side.

"You've checked my seat?" he reiterated.

Her mouth twitched but she kept facing forward. "It's one of my favourite things about you."

With that, she was off again, a snicker and a trot and they burst from the copse to find themselves atop a ridge. Matilda pulled to a halt, and Henri—with Beryl's tacit help—pulled up beside her.

Henri wondered if she had any clue that she was humming; some song or other, or a tune that only she knew. It was something she did when she was feeling contented.

"We run the land as far as the eye can see. Saltbush and mallee scrub, rocky hills, sudden ravines, and shady canyons. Hectares of flat grazing lands marked by well-kept fences and neat cattle grids and dams filled with bore water or river water. We've all got the kind of water rights our neighbours would give up a kidney to get their hands on."

She resettled her hat with its wonky rim a little further back on her head. The glow of the setting sun painted a vibrant pink and orange haze on the horizon, making her blue eyes appear even brighter than usual.

"Pretty great, don't you think?" she asked, a smile tugging at the corners of her uptilted lips.

"I'm not sure I've seen anything more beautiful," he said.

A grin lit her face as she turned. It faltered when she saw his eyes were only on her.

"Henri," she chastised. But her eyes softened. Her gaze tracing the edges of his face.

With no need to be subtle here, or feel concern that some servant or citizen might notice his lingering gaze, Henri drank her in. Boldly. Blatantly. As if this place demanded it.

If the Matilda he'd known all those years ago had been a burst of joy, and the Matilda who'd popped up on the street in Côte de Lapis had been an extraordinary disruptor, Matilda Waverly on home soil was nothing short of transcendental.

"Rose can't give up this place, Henri," she said, her expression no longer sunshine and light. "It's her lifeblood."

"Could you?" he wondered, and then when her eyes widened he realised he'd said it out loud.

At least he hadn't said what he was really wondering, which was, *Could you give it up for me?*

Another reason why he'd had to come. So that he would be under no illusion as to all that he'd be asking her to leave behind if things worked out the way he was beginning to expect they might.

"Come on," she said, her voice soft as she

turned her horse on the spot and nudged him back toward the Homestead.

Early the next morning, Matilda sat on the back porch of her childhood home, laptop open to the book she'd been working on, cupping a mug of cooling coffee, legs curled up on her favourite chair, a mohair blanket tucked around her legs, River snoring gently at her feet.

Ready for when Henri might stumble bleary-eyed from his room, the way she had after collapsing in a heap her first night in the château.

Till then, she soaked in the crisp wintry air. The earthy scents. The sky that went on forever.

If the front of the Homestead was a showpiece often featured in articles about the great homes of Australia, the veranda by the back door, with its older furniture, the view through gaps in the watery grey of the ghost gums to stockyards, sheds the size of airplane hangars, was the working heart of the Downs, where they truly lived.

And yet, despite how familiar it all was, how ruggedly beautiful, whether it was Rose's "vision board" text, or the amount of time she'd spent away, Matilda felt a kind of disconnect.

"You all right, Tilly?"

Matilda turned to find Lindy, their housekeeper, standing at the top of the back steps by the big, dented metal bell. It harked back to generations gone when it had been used to call in hungry workers with a holler of, "Grub's up!" The girls had known the sound as their signal to cease whatever mischief they were up to and come inside.

"Sorry, Lindy," Matilda said, "did I wake you?"

"Not at all. Plenty to do in a house this size, even if the rooms are mostly empty these days. And now you're back, there's more cooking and cleaning for sure."

Matilda went to laugh, to make some joke, falling into her happy-happy joy-joy role as easily as sliding into old slippers. But instead stopped herself and said, "Can I help?"

"I'm all good. Now, can I get *you* anything?"

Matilda held up her coffee. "I'm covered."

"And your...friend?" Lindy asked. "Does he need anything?"

Matilda had introduced Lindy and Henri when they'd come in from their ride.

Once Lindy had herded him into the green guest room, to "wash off the day," Lindy had asked Matilda if she was absolutely sure there wasn't enough space in her *own* large bedroom for such a dashing friend.

"As far as I know Henri is still gone to the world," said Matilda. "If he rouses himself anytime soon, can you tell him where I am?"

Lindy nodded. Then, with a glorious sigh, went back inside.

Leaving Matilda to watch the winter sun melting the frost from the grass and the station stir-ring, and think about this place. What it meant. And what they might all be willing to do to pro-tect it.

The way Eve had been acting since the read-ing of the will, as if she'd somehow *known* about the affair... Would she actually care if Garrison Downs was lost? Matilda was certain that deep down she would.

Then there was Ana, who had no connection to the place at all. Yet she could. If they managed to pull this off, what an amazing opportunity it would be for them to cement their sisterhood.

And then there was wonderful, hardworking, caring Rose, for whom Garrison Downs was her life's dream.

Matilda looked toward the back door, think-ing her way to where Henri slept. And she knew, even if this place wasn't what *she* wanted any-more, she'd still go a long way to protect it for those she loved.

"Tilly?"

Matilda coughed on her Vegemite toast, as she turned to find Rose moseying into the kitchen an hour later, covered in dirt from head to toe. She threw down her toast and ran to her sister, envel-oping her in a hug.

"Hey!" said Rose, laughing, her arms out to

the sides. "Are you sure you want to be doing that. I reek."

"You smell perfect."

Rose gave her a quick squeeze before peeling herself free, then heading to the fridge for a half bottle of orange juice, which she downed in one go.

"What are you doing back?" Rose asked.

It gave Matilda the perfect opening to say, "If Lindy hasn't spilled the beans as yet, I brought a visitor."

Rose stopped drinking.

"He's in the green guest room. Twenty bucks says he's still face down on the bed, snoring."

"He?"

"Yes, *he*."

"And he's a snorer?"

"Well, no, that was just a figure of—" Matilda snapped her mouth shut at Rose's quick smile.

Though it was quickly followed by a frown, brimming with big sisterly concern. "And there I was thinking you've been spending your days staring down musty paintings and gorging on Nutella crepes."

"Sorry," said Matilda. "I wanted to wait for the right time to tell you. So as not to worry you."

Rose cocked a hip against the bench. "Ought I be worried now?"

"About Henri? On the contrary." Then, "But there's more."

Matilda told her. How they'd met, how they'd adventured, how they'd said "I do." Rose's face remained impassive until Matilda mentioned their mother, and a finger lifted to press against her lips.

"After Dad's will, I had to find out. In case our situation satisfies the condition."

"Oh, Tilly—"

"There's more still," Matilda said, holding out a staying hand. "You might want to sit down for this next bit."

Rose levelled her with a look. Before turning to click on the kettle.

"Fine. But I warned you. His name is Henri Gaultier Raphael-Rossetti. And he is a prince. But not just any prince, the Sovereign Prince of Chaleur."

After a few beats, Rose said, "Well, I'm glad he's not just *any* prince. If so, I'd have said to put him in the lilac guest room."

Matilda blinked. "You are being very blasé about this."

Rose popped a tea bag into a mug with the Marni Cup logo on the side. "That's because I know."

"*What* do you know?"

Rose pulled the band from her ponytail, then retied it, a sign she wasn't as cool about all this as she was making out to be. "Eve told me."

"*Eve?*"

"After you called her and left a cryptic message about—let me see if I have this straight—*kissing a prince who might be your husband*, she called me to give me a right bollocking. How could I have let this happen?"

While it hurt that Eve hadn't called *her*, and while it must have been a tense phone call, Matilda was glad they'd at least spoken.

"My actions are not your fault. Or your concern."

"I think," said Rose, "it's the thought of our little sister out there, trying to save us all. That's what I was trying to say the other day. This is not your responsibility. We are not your responsibility. We will find another way."

"And if we don't?"

Rose looked at her then, not as a *little* sister, but as a sister in arms. "You do realise, even if by some miracle you end up with a marriage certificate in hand, Eve and I would have to magically find ourselves husbands as well."

"And Ana," said Matilda. "Don't forget Ana."

"How could I forget Ana!" Rose asked, hands flailing, before she regathered herself. "Sorry. That came out more harshly than I meant."

Rose blew out an exasperated breath before she put down the mug, came to Matilda, and wrapped her in her dusty, dirty, wonderful arms. "Tell me about him, so I can be forewarned."

"Henri?"

"Yes, Henri, unless you have a duke stashed here somewhere too."

"Ha-ha. Well, he's…he's lovely. Smart, and generous. Stubborn, determined, works too hard. Shy, I think, a little. Or introverted, maybe. He's well-read, loves Whitman. He's better at the wheel than he is in the saddle. He's open-minded, but strong in his convictions. And he's working hard to make his country the best place it can be."

"And he's awake." That from Lindy, who'd appeared at the kitchen door. "I heard the shower going in his room just now. Sorry, you asked if I could let you know."

"Thanks, Lindy," Matilda said, standing straight as her nerves switched on one by one at the thought of seeing him again.

"And you left out *gorgeous*," Lindy stage-whispered. Then to Rose, she said, "Just you wait and see."

Rose raised an eyebrow Matilda's way.

"Fine, yes, Henri is gorgeous. If you're into tall, dark, built, stupidly handsome royal types."

"*Meh…*" said Rose. Then, "That's a lot of nice things you had to say about the guy. Is it possible that you have feelings for him?"

"Rose," she said, feeling heat sweep into her cheeks.

"Is it?"

"I did love him, once upon a time."

Saying the words out loud, Matilda felt the

rush of them. As if the feelings were freshly laundered. Clean, crisp, and bright.

Not that it mattered. It wasn't the point. Taking into consideration distance, duty, backgrounds, responsibilities, challenges they couldn't hope to foresee—love was complicated under *normal* circumstances. Add the situation in which her family had found itself, and who he was, and it would be a disaster.

"I'm going to shower," said Rose, checking her watch, "then head back out, so if I don't get to meet your prince among men in the hall now, I will see you at dinner. Okay?"

"Done."

Matilda found Henri in the hall.

He had showered, dark finger tracks ran through his hair, a Superman curl swishing across his brow. His cheeks had pinked in the cool air, contradicting the hard angles of his jaw. And rather than his usual smart suit, he wore jeans, a thick woollen jumper, and boots, his adorable attempt at farm chic.

"Morning, sunshine," she said, belying the thumpity-thump of her heart that had begun when Rose had asked if she loved him and was yet to subside. "Hungry?"

"Ravenous."

She handed him a piece of Vegemite toast and

watched him muscle his way through it as if it wasn't offending every single one of his taste buds.

"I was going to take a walk," she said. "Want to join me?"

"So long as you never make me eat whatever that was ever again, I'll follow you anywhere."

It was a line, meaningless, and yet it lodged in her chest like an arrow.

Seriously, Tilly, get a grip.

"Warm enough?" she asked, when they stepped outside.

"This is balmy compared with winter back home. When we get snows, we get *snows*, the mountaintops covered, the aspens laden. You think Chaleur beautiful now, you should see it come Christmastime."

She opened her mouth to ask if that was an invitation, then remembered herself.

They spent a lazy morning ambling around the Homestead grounds, meandering past the Old House, staying clear of the Settlers Cottage due to its ghosts and mega snakes and all the things that had made it out-of-bounds when they were kids.

And Matilda tried her best *not* to think about the feelings she was feeling for Henri. Not when he stopped, breathed in deeply, and marvelled over the clarity of the air. Or when he reached out to take her hand to help her jump over a fallen tree.

Not even when he begged to spend the afternoon in his room, which had its own small lounge and desk with a view, like every guest room in the Homestead, to "check in." And didn't demur when she set herself up on an upholstered chair in the corner of his suite to work on her book while he worked at running a country. For it had become their ritual, that's all.

After one phone call that left him rubbing both hands over his face and into his hair, she said, "Tell me something you *like* about being prince."

He looked to her and laughed. A real laugh, loose and trusting and free. The sound moved through her like liquid heat.

"I was asked the same question recently by a second grader and I struggled to find an answer."

"It has to be the fervid adoration, though, right? Like that day on the street in Côte de Lapis? *'Henri, je t'aime!' 'So handsome, Henri!' 'You were always my favourite, Henri.'*"

He twisted in his chair so he was facing her. "So, I *am* your favourite. I did wonder."

"Pfft," she said, "you're like third, maybe fourth, on my list. There's Prince Charming. Prince Caspian. Flynn Rider becomes a prince when he marries Rapunzel, right? Straight to number one."

Henri smiled the smile of a man who knew better.

How? How did he know? Was it obvious that some switch had been flipped since coming home? That while her defences had been down, her sister had asked her a simple question and she'd turned to jelly.

"Your turn," he said. "What did you love most about growing up here?"

"Compared to what you've told me about your childhood, I might seem like I'm showing off."

"Try me," he said.

When Matilda realised what he was doing—asking the questions he knew he *should* have asked her back then—she capitulated.

"Fine," said Matilda, putting her laptop aside. "It was bliss. Surrounded by animals and trees to climb and staff who felt like family. Our father…" Her heart bucked. "He was built for running this place. Physically tough, financially savvy, quietly charismatic. While our mother was elegant, fiercely loving. She couldn't wait to see how we all turned out."

"She'd be very proud. I'd bet a kingdom."

Matilda lifted her eyes to his, to find a brimming intensity in his gaze. "If only you *had* a kingdom, not a mere principality."

"Alas." Henri smiled. His eyes midnight dark and so focused on her Matilda could barely breathe.

Why did you really make me bring you here? she wanted to ask.

If he said, *Because I adore you now as I adored you then, and it broke my heart to see you go, and if I'd only known how to find you I would have come on wings of fire*, while she sat in the house her father's guilt had built, she wasn't sure she could trust that it mattered.

And if he said anything other than those words, her poor reanimated heart might never recover.

Then the bell at the back door rang across the Downs.

"What on earth—" Henri said, flinching in his chair.

Matilda laughed, the tension releasing from her body a blessed relief.

"That'll be Rose calling us in for dinner. Ready to meet my sister?"

Henri stood and ran both hands down the sides of his jeans, as if he was nervous to meet Rose. And if that wasn't her favourite moment of the trip home so far, she couldn't say what was.

"Come on, Your Highness. Let's get this over with." She slid her hand into the crook of Henri's arm and led him unto the breach.

CHAPTER EIGHT

DINNER WAS…INTERESTING.

Lindy—having created a veritable feast in Henri's honour—nearly tripped over her tongue when Henri stood to help her carry the Waverly roast beef to the table.

While Rose made sure Henri knew the entirety of Chaleur could fit into Garrison Downs ten times over. Though Matilda watched her slowly become #TeamHenri when he asked salient questions about their stud stock and her favourite brand of tractor.

When Rose finally excused herself, claiming the need for an early night, she shot Matilda a glance to say, *Fine. He's lovely. But I'm just down the hall, and I know where to hide bodies.*

Matilda, too buzzed to go to bed, offered Henri a tour of the house proper. And Henri accepted.

"And this," said Matilda, as she stepped through a large doorway, "was my father's office."

The banker's lamp on the desk was on low, the lamp by her mother's chair in the back corner glowing softly. Both on a timer that switched them on every day at four in the afternoon.

It had never occurred to Matilda why that was, it had simply been. But now, with both her parents gone, and her version of their romantic history all muddled in her head, she realised *her father* must have kept it going after her mother had died. A reminder of his wife every single day.

"You okay?" Henri asked.

She blinked away the sheen in her eyes. "This room, it holds a lot of memories."

"Rooms can do that," he said, squeezing her arm gently as he swept by.

And she realised as she watched him move about the room, the warm light playing over his features, that he did understand. In fact, he might understand *her* in a way no one else ever would. Her sisters included.

Those crisp fresh feelings that had come over her in the kitchen that morning rose up again. She tried swallowing them down, but they would not be stopped.

She'd loved this man once, fiercely, with her entire being. And while he had changed, at his core he was the same kind, patient, inquisitive, warm, secure man.

Despite the fact her belief in forever love had been shaken, so much so that the book she had been working on so furiously of late was a collation of letters from *doomed* love affairs, was it possible that she—with time, with care, with courage—could really feel that way again?

He looked up. Caught her gaze. Raised an eyebrow in question.

"Look at this," she said, grabbing the remote from the coffee table in a panic. She moved to the centre of the room to show Henri how the artwork at the back of the room slid into a cavity in the ceiling to reveal a large screen her father had used for important video calls. "Pretty snazzy, huh?"

Henri's smile was warm. As if he knew exactly why she was babbling. And Matilda's heart twisted when it hit her how much she'd have loved to have introduced Henri to her dad. And her mother too. They'd have spoken fast French and debated politics. Her mother would have *loved* him.

Maybe, just maybe, that was the thing that hurt most of all. Not the secrets or the lies, but the fact her parents were gone. Gone before she'd had the chance to really know them. Before they had the chance to truly know her.

"This desk," said Henri, dragging Matilda back to the present. "It's Dutch?"

"A gift from the Royal House of the Netherlands in fact. Do you know them?"

"Rather well," Henri said with a smile.

"They're big fans of Dad's grain-fed beef."

"How old?" Henri asked, bending to take in the details.

"Two hundred years, give or take."

"Two hundred, you say?" He ran his finger along the edge of the desk. Then he dropped to a crouch to look more closely. Before his gaze lifted to hers. "Come here."

It took half a second for Matilda to realise what he'd found, and she was at his side in a heartbeat.

He took her hand, guiding it till she felt the catch. A hidden locked drawer. Right there, for anyone who knew where to look.

Matilda opened her mouth to call for Rose. Or for Lindy to go find Rose. Then stopped. She needed this. Needed answers. Needed some connection to her father that existed outside of the damn will.

Grabbing a letter opener, she jammed the thing in the hidden lock and jiggled till some part of the mechanism snapped.

Heart beating in her throat, she yanked the drawer open. And inside... It was the mother lode. In every way. For this drawer belonged to Rosamund.

Flicking through the pile of papers, she found her mother's will, including reference to the generous trust funds she had bestowed on her three daughters. Cards the girls had written to her—birthday, Christmas, Mother's Day.

And all the letters Matilda had sent. From

boarding school, from university, from the summer she'd gone away. The summer her mum had been unwell and not told a soul, knowing it would bring Matilda home.

Matilda's hand shook as it lifted to her mouth, to stop the sob gathering there.

"Matilda?" Henri said, his hand gentle at her back, his voice raw as if seeing her upset was cutting him to pieces. "Can I get someone? Can I do anything?"

"Stay." She reached back and held Henri's hand where it was. A lifeline. Essential. As she realised, like the lamp in the corner, her father had kept her mother's papers, near, right till the end. That *was* love. She was *certain* of it.

"Medical records," Matilda said as she pulled a thick folder with tattered corners and yellowed papers from the bottom of the drawer.

"From that summer?" Henri asked, moving in beside her. Cocooning her in his warmth. His support.

Matilda shook her head. "Several months after I was born."

Matilda's heart beat heavily as she skimmed terms such as self-harm, ideation, postpartum psychosis. And a long hospital stay.

"Oh," she said on an outshot of breath. Her mother had suffered terribly from postnatal depression after she had been born. For months, by the look of things, before a diagnosis came through. Around the time her father had had his affair.

Her fingers numb from shock, the pages spilled to the floor. She followed, dropping to her knees. Her hand landing on a notebook with a red leather cover, soft and aged. The edges of the pages were dusted in gold, her mother's initials embossed in the lower right corner.

Not a notebook. A *journal*.

Matilda turned and leaned against her father's desk. The solid wood keeping her upright.

She opened the book to find the first entry, written in her mother's long looping hand. Black ink, never blue.

I write these words upon instruction from experts who seem to believe it will help. I write these words so that I might find my way back to my daughters, my life, myself. I write these words to commit to my circumstances, and to bend them to suit my needs, the needs of my girls, and the needs of my family. I write these words as I choose to flourish, and no longer to fade.

Tears running down her face before she got to the bottom of the page, Matilda read on. Immersed in her mother's beautiful, painfully honest tales of her first few years at the Downs. How stunning she'd found it, and how isolating.

She wrote of how unexpectedly raw and deep she found her love for her daughters, and how bleak it had felt when those feelings did not come. How she had worn her husband to a nub as he had tried to "fix things." Wanting nothing of him. Until he turned to another woman's arms.

Until one day she saw past her homesickness to know this was deeper. The disconnection from her youngest, with her sweet nature and her husband's bright eyes, was nonsensical. Once a diagnosis had been made, Holt had been there. At her side the entire time. Promising that if she was back, so was he. Promises that had saved their family. Their life.

Throat clogged, her face damp with tears, Matilda closed the book and held it to her heart.

In trying to understand how her parents' love had been so fractured, she'd been looking in the wrong place. Blaming her father for making a wretched choice. This journal, this unfurling of pain, pressed onto the pages like flowers between the pages of a heavy book, showed a different truth. That circumstance had come at them, hard. And they'd beat it back. Together.

Matilda looked up to find Henri crouched by her, his hands over his mouth, his gaze on her. As if her pain was his pain.

She sobbed, choking on her breath, as the last vestiges of control she had over her feelings imploded. And she felt it all. Rage, sorrow, joy, love, hurt, disappointment, forgiveness.

Then Henri was beside her. Sitting on the floor of her father's office, running a hand over her hair, making soft cooing noises, and speaking in deep sonorous French, while she curled herself into his chest and cried.

After leaving Matilda with Rose—the sisters needing to deal with the revelations in their mother's journal together—Henri made his way to his room. And lay there, staring at the ceiling, his body aching with a kind of psychic pain, after seeing Matilda in such distress.

It was near three by the time his eyes finally drifted closed, only to jolt awake when he heard music.

He pushed back the covers, rubbed both hands over his face, then, still dressed in the jeans and woollen sweater he'd worn to dinner, followed the sound to find a room of plush white carpet, an elegant bar at one end, a piano in the centre.

Moonlight poured through the large French windows, sparking off a chandelier before dappling Matilda's hair and shoulders as she sat behind the instrument, her fingers trailing over the keys, playing something simple, slow, sweet, and haunting.

When he moved into the room, she looked up. Her eyes red, her expression raw.

"Did I wake you?"

"I couldn't sleep." Henri moved toward her, watching her fingers run silently over the keys. "What were you playing?"

"Nothing, really. Our mother wanted us to have lessons, culture being under her purview. I lasted about six months, got to the point that I could play 'The Entertainer,' and was done."

Henri noted the loose T-shirt draping off one shoulder, the striped flannel pyjama bottoms with a hole in the thigh, the fluffy socks on her feet. She looked so rumpled and warm he wanted to scoop her up and take her back to bed. His bed. Where he could take care of her, soothe her, make her feel better all night long.

The fact he'd been fighting the same desire for days, *weeks*, and had managed to not voice it so succinctly inside his own head, said something about the decision-making properties of three in the morning.

Instead, he looked to the pile of letters sitting haphazardly atop the piano. "What are they?"

"From my mother's drawer. The letters I wrote when I was traveling. I wanted to see if I had ever mentioned you."

His gaze lifted to hers, but she was ruffling through the papers before handing him one. And as he read, her voice leaped off the page. Pure joy and light as she told a tale of art and music, falling snow, and train rides through tunnels that went on forever. And at the bottom a PS.

I kind of met someone, Mum. It's been a bit of a whirlwind (sound familiar?) but I just know you'll love him too.

Henri read that final sentence a few times over, absorbing Matilda's certainty, after only a few days of knowing him, that she'd one day bring him home.

He folded the letter and handed it back to her. "Move over," he said, motioning with a nod for her to make room on the bench.

Her breath hitched, a shudder running through her, when his arm rubbed against hers. Her emotions erratic. But then she stayed, leaning there against him.

"Can you play?" she asked.

"Can I play," he scoffed gently. Then he lined up his fingers and banged out an enthusiastic version of chopsticks.

Matilda's fingers closed over his, drawing them to her chest. "Shush!" she said, laughing. "You'll wake Rose and Lindy!"

Henri looked toward the door, chagrined. "Are their rooms near?"

"Other side of the house. And my sister sleeps like the dead."

When he looked to her, her eyes were luminous

in the moonlight. She shifted his hand so it nestled over her heart. And he knew he could have kissed her then. Taking up where they'd left off in the library. He knew he could touch her, hold her, taste her, lose himself in her as he'd once done. Back when losing himself had been his sole goal in life.

Only now the thought of losing himself felt like a forfeit.

He wanted to own his time. To do hard things and do them well. To consume life, to make a difference.

And despite the ache in his chest every time he looked at Matilda, for so much of this new focus he felt was because of her, he knew she was in a far more fragile place. And that he had to take care.

Not that she seemed to agree, for she lifted his hand, placed her lips on a knuckle. When he did not object, she kissed her way along them all. Her tongue swiping along the final dip, sending a shard of heat right to his core.

Then she uncurled his fingers and lifted his hand to cup her cheek. And she leaned into his touch, sighing, as if all the big feelings that had been flooding through her finally had somewhere to go.

Perhaps that's what he could be for her? The vessel into which she could pour her pain. He *could* take it. He could take it all.

Breathing out, he traced the dark smudge beneath her eye with the pad of his thumb. Then the furrow above her nose. Then he leaned in and pressed a gentle kiss to her forehead. And closed his eyes so that he could absorb her warmth, her soft scent, the energy always coursing just below the surface.

"You should get some sleep," he murmured against her skin.

"I don't want sleep. I want to be right here. With you."

And his heart began to beat a steady tattoo. *Mine…mine…mine…mine.*

"Matilda," he said, his voice rough. "It's been a hell of a day."

"Henri," she returned, his name a breath. A *wish.* "It's been a hell of a few years. But having you here, finally, and knowing that you never saw my note, that you didn't cut me free as if I had meant nothing…"

His jaw tightened to the point of pain. "Matilda—"

She cut him off. "You know I've been tinkering with a book the past couple of weeks, right? I've actually been collating material for it for years. Letters. Hundreds of letters. The theme: doomed love affairs. *That's* how I've been choosing to expend my creative energy, trying to convince other people that love sucks."

She sniffed out a sorry laugh. "But that's not

who I am. It's not who I want to be. I want—I want—"

Then, before she said another word, she grabbed him by the sweater, pulled him to her and kissed him. Hard. Her eyes closed tight, as if the *connection* was everything. As if she might expire without it.

After a long, loaded beat, Henri pulled away. A last chance to be rational. But the sound she made, the moan of displeasure at the lack of him, was like a siren call. And he knew he was done for.

His hand delved into her hair and when he kissed her again, a soft slow slide of mouths, everything deepened, softened. She mewled, moving against him, and he knew that if there was a single forfeit he could abide, it was to her.

Her arms slid around his neck and with one smooth move, she lifted off the stool and straddled him. Her back brushing the keys, creating a jangle of notes. The dissonance a hastening thing, a soundtrack to the feelings building quickly inside of him, cacophonous, unchecked.

The hand at her neck tugged her T-shirt over one shoulder to reveal the swell of her breast. The thin cotton catching on the uptilted sweep of her nipple, a shadow of colour. Pure temptation. He traced her collarbone with open-mouthed kisses and moved to the curve of her breast.

Matilda rolled into him. Then again. Both feeling too much and not enough.

If he had learned patience, it was in preparation for this very moment. The slow millimetres, eking out her pleasure, tasting her, relearning her tells. While Matilda, impatient as ever, chased connection, begged for relief in every shift of her body, every ragged breath expelled from her lungs.

And soon Henri was running the high wire between adrenaline and exhaustion, desire and care. Till she leaned back against the piano, draped over the thing. The growl he emitted at the sight of her, had her eyes blinking open, dreamy, only half there. And then she smiled, as if she knew exactly what she did to him. The control she could wield if she so chose.

And just like that, fear slipped into the cracks where regret had long lived. Fear that every day they spent together was a day closer to a time when they would have to part, and this dreamy expression would haunt his dreams for years to come.

Matilda curled herself back into his embrace. And she lifted her hand to trace his forehead. "You are thinking so hard right now."

He didn't deny it. Though when her hand disappeared into the back of his hair, caressing, soothing, tugging, he couldn't remember why he'd been thinking anything at all.

He saw the cotton still snagged on her nipple and ran his thumb over the shadow. When he did it again, she followed his touch. He leaned her back again so that he could suck the cotton into his mouth, taking the skin beneath between his teeth, and a ragged sigh escaped her mouth.

When it became too much—the constriction of the hard seat and piano—he pressed the stool back. It resisted against the plush carpet, so he kicked it away, and it fell with a dull thud.

Then he lifted Matilda onto the piano proper, her feet landing gently on the keys in a tinkle of sound. Her hair fell over her shoulders in messy waves, catching on her tangled lashes.

His hands, full of the cotton of her shirt, pressed into her waist. Then lifted, slowly, dragging her T-shirt with them, until he finally found skin, warm and lush. Pinked with desire. He tilted her right back until her head landed gently on the piano lid, her back arched, her toes playing notes he'd never forget.

He shucked her shirt higher and pressed his face to her belly. Circling her navel with his tongue before lapping at the dip, again and again as her body began to tremble. His hand holding her in place, he kissed his way along the low rise of her soft pyjama bottoms. Scraped his teeth along the edge of her hip bone. Low enough to catch the scent of her.

As if she could feel the feral rising inside of

him, she sat up just enough to whip her shirt over her head, reaching for him, saying, "Please, Henri." Before she began clawing at his sweater.

His gaze caught on hers, the universe therein. "I didn't stop to grab any protection when I followed the sound of your song."

She winced, then laughed. "I wasn't exactly planning this either." Then she lay back, her head hitting the piano lid with another light thud.

Matilda. Naked to the waist. This was not a problem so far as he saw it. A world of ways he might pleasure her crashed over him, like waves on a stormy coastline.

He started by tracing a small scar beneath her left breast with his thumb, then followed it with a kiss. He caressed the lower incline of her breast, watching the way goose bumps sprang up in its wake. He followed the path of the flush that washed across her skin with the flat of his hand, then the rise of her ribs, the gentle mound of her belly.

When she gasped and bit down on her bottom lip, arching into his touch, he took advantage. Hooking his fingers into the soft elastic of her pants, he tugged them down her legs, over her feet, in one swoop, then tossed them over his shoulder.

An arm thrown over her eyes, her knees bobbed together and separated. Fretting. Teasing.

Till with a sweep of his thumb, he tugged her

underwear aside and ran his nose up her centre, his tongue following with a long flat sweep. And she bucked against him, her breath leaving her in a gasp.

"More?" he asked, his voice rough.

"More," she begged, letting her knees go. And when her hands moved to his hair, tugging, directing, he took her legs, swinging them over his shoulders, and went to town.

The taste of her, the heat, the way she quivered under his ministrations—he could have lived in that place, holding her on the edge, savouring her pleasure for the rest of his natural life.

Her hands gripped his hair, her body restless, gasping, and open, until she lifted her hips to his mouth, her legs spilling outward, strained, a goddess in his arms. Before her breath caught, and time stopped for several long perfect seconds, before she shuddered around him.

Saying his name, sobbing it over and over again, till he felt her pleasure and her pain, her relief and her release. As if it had been inevitable.

When she whispered his name, just the once, on a long outward breath, he kissed her once more, saving his place, before he gently pressed her knees together and let her feet lower to the keys, where they scattered another low sweet tune. Then he circled his hand over her belly, chasing the quivers that kept going and going and going.

Eventually, she let her arms fall to the side, and she huffed out a laugh. Then another. Then laughed till she could scarce draw breath.

"That's not the reaction I was hoping for," he said.

She shot him a heart-stopping grin. "I was just thinking we were never even allowed to wear *shoes* in here." Then she laughed again.

With that, she rolled gracefully off the piano. Landing on legs that near gave way, thanks to him. Then she turned to him, all but naked, flushed, ruffled, and absolutely beautiful. Then held out her hand. "You coming?"

"You tell me," he rumbled.

"The Prince has a mouth on him," she said. Before a shiver racked through her. "Yes, he does."

He took her hand as she led him out of the room, finding it hard to walk, considering the hard-on pressed against the zipper of his jeans. His entire body was wound tight as drum.

She gathered up her clothes as they passed. Then over her shoulder said, "I'm really glad you're here, Henri."

No matter what happened from here on in, Henri was too.

Early the next day Matilda crept out of her bedroom, a blanket tossed over her T-shirt and pyjama pants, and padded into the kitchen.

With sunlight filtering gently through the skylight, angling shards of cream over the muted whites of the Hamptons style space, she made herself a quick piece of toast, then set her laptop up on the bench and opened a brand-new file.

The doomed love affair book was going on the backburner. She was filled with too many new ideas, lush ideas, of collections of letters with redemption themes or reunions, the kind that uplifted and gave people hope.

Rose walked into the kitchen and put her morning coffee cup in the sink.

Yawning, Matilda said, "Morning."

Rose looked to Matilda, her gaze still a little raw after the hours they'd spent going over the journal the night before. "Feeling better?"

Matilda put a hand under her chin. "Much. I promise. You?"

"Better," Rose agreed. "Your handsome prince still asleep?"

"I assume so," said Matilda around her toast. She'd left him face down, naked in her bed, his beautiful arms tucked under his pillow, the dark sweep of his hair falling across his cheek. If she wasn't so famished, she'd have climbed right back in.

Rose laughed into her coffee. "You have *the* worst poker face. If it was you trying to win Garrison Downs in that poker game, we'd have been screwed." Then, "But you really are feeling better?"

Matilda gave Rose the benefit of a beat of

thought. "I really am. It's a lot—the journal, the medical records, learning Mum had had post-natal depressions after she had *me*. But it's also a relief to have some inkling as to why things went the way they went."

"Mmm," said Rose, something in her expression making Matilda sure *she* wasn't quite so ready to let things go. But she'd get there, Matilda was sure of it.

"Though there is one thing," said Matilda, "that is stuck in my craw. Do you *remember* any of it? Remember them fighting when we were little? Because I honestly don't remember a harsh word. Unless Dad walked dirt through the house, but then he'd make Mum laugh or pull her in for a quick kiss and disarm her into forgiving him."

Rose, older than Matilda by a few years, said, "It was definitely different in the Old House. We were all crammed in, with Nanna and Pop, living on top of one another. Things improved once we moved in here." Then Rose's expression changed. "Why do you ask? Did you and Henri fight?"

Matilda *pffted*. "This has nothing to do with us."

Well, it did. A little. Okay a lot, actually. But not the way Rose imagined. More that she wondered if she was the way she was—leaping about, making sure everyone else was happy, avoiding conflict at all costs—because of how things had been when she was young.

"So there is an *us*," said Rose.

Matilda had to backtrack to get her meaning. "What? No."

"Tilly, the guy followed you here, from La Whoop-Whoop. I think *he* thinks there's an 'us.' So if you don't, then you might want to be careful."

Careful? After the night they'd spent together more than making up for lost time, it was a bit late for that. She'd never play the piano again without coming out in a sweat.

"It's *fine*," Matilda insisted. "We're on the same page. We both know the deal."

The reasons they were together, after all, had not changed. Despite the new intimacies, the long walks, the deep conversations. Despite a night so raw and tender and true, they were not *together* in any definable way.

As for the indefinable… It *was* different than before. Less whirlwind, more anchored. As if time, age, experience, heartache, and loss made them aware of the rarity and the fragility of what they'd once had.

As to what they had now—

"Tilly." Rose motioned to Matilda's mobile, buzzing at her elbow.

Saved by the phone, she said, "It's Ana."

After a beat, Matilda answered. "Hey, Ana Banana!"

Rose's eyes widened. Okay, so maybe that was a little much.

"Tilly?" said Ana after a long beat, her voice breathless. Then, "Sorry, I think I pocket-dialled you."

"All good. Where are you?"

"I'm at the dawn markets with my mother, picking out fresh fruit and vegetables for my grandparents' restaurant. At dawn."

"The things we do for family," she said, shooting Rose a look. Rose poked out her tongue.

"Any news regards the will?" Ana asked, her voice softer, as if she'd found an alcove somewhere.

"Rose would know. I'll put you on speaker." Rose waved a wild hand at Matilda, but it was too late.

"Hi, Rose," said Ana.

"Hi, Ana," said Rose. Then, her face scrunching, said, "Nothing new."

"Well, hopefully a plan will present itself."

Matilda pointed at her own chest and mouthed, *See*.

Rose shook her head slowly. Then she motioned that she was going to head off. Duty called. The station waited for no woman.

"Sorry," said Ana, "I have to go. My mother is a fast walker, and I'll lose her in the arugula section if I'm not careful."

Once they'd rung off, Matilda gave up on her

book, made herself a coffee, then went to find somewhere to sit so she could call Eve. If voice messages got through to her, then that's what she was about to get. A barrage, starting with news of their mother's journal.

But when Matilda reached the back door, she saw Rose had only made her way as far as the tree swing in the back yard. Their dad had built it when they were younger—a plank of wood, hanging by chain from the branch of a big old gum tree, the seat just big enough to fit the three of them, even now.

The swing moved gently as if with the motion of the wind as Rose looked out over the gardens and beyond them to where the morning sun painted swathes of the most brilliant colours across the wispiest of clouds.

Then Rose lifted a hand and—

Had she just wiped a *tear*? Surely not.

Matilda watched, unblinking, and… There! Rose wiped the back of her hand across her cheek before tipping forward, her face landing in her hands as her shoulders moved in wracking sobs.

Oh, no. Oh, *Rose*. Matilda *knew*; it wasn't about their mum's journal. Rose had worked her way through that the night before. It was about Garrison Downs. About Ana. About the damn lawyer. About the gargantuan task ahead of them if they were to tie this up.

It was a much-needed reminder of why she was

there—to show Henri what she was fighting for, so that when the time came to make a decision, it would take a harder man than he to deny her.

CHAPTER NINE

HENRI WOKE TO sunshine pouring through pale blue curtains. Book quotes framed in rustic frames on bright white walls. It took a beat to remember where he was, till he rolled over and caught Matilda's scent on the empty pillow beside his.

And the night came back to him. Every glorious moment.

Grinning like a fool, he sat up, his feet pressed into the carpet, and ruffled a hand through his messy hair. He grabbed his phone to find missed call after missed call from Andre.

He'd been letting his cousin sweat while also letting his cousin's words percolate. For while Andre's method of saving him from himself had been indefensible, he hadn't been altogether wrong.

Matilda's life till that point had been so cloistered, and Henri had not been in the mental space to make such a big life choice. Getting to know one another, as adults, these past weeks had been a slower, deeper, richer experience. One he could not bring himself to regret.

His phone buzzed. A message from Celeste. He opened it to read:

Celeste: Your Highness. Prince Andre has been in touch, querying if, and I quote, "there might be adequate enough internet service in the back of beyond so that he might engage you in a video conference call."

Henri laughed before he could stop himself, his cousin's tone clear as a bell. And he decided Andre had been in the doghouse long enough. Then Celeste's next message came through and the laughter turned to dust in his mouth.

Celeste: Your Highness. Prince Andre now says to let you know that he has a result on the mission you commanded him to undertake.

This was it.

Whatever Andre had uncovered, after this everything would change. A plan would be put in motion. Promises made and kept, so as to ensure the faith and happiness of his nation, which he had come to discover truly mattered to him.

For he had promised to be their prince. To work to uphold their values and needs. And that had to be his guiding light.

He showered quickly, dressed, then went looking for Matilda, finding her lying on a chair on the back porch, a blanket over her shoulders, her arm flung over her eyes. River panting happily on the floor beside her.

"Matilda," he said, quietly.

She lifted her arm and squinted. Then made to sit up. All flapping arms and messy hair, the mark from the cushion she'd been lying on pressed endearingly into her cheek.

"Henri," she said. "Sorry. I must have fallen asleep."

The reason why flickered through his mind like an old movie. Henri cleared his throat. "Last night, you showed me the screen in your father's office, the one he used for video calls."

"I did? I *did*. That feels like a hundred years ago."

"Andre has been in touch asking if we can conference in. He has news."

"News?" she asked, mid-stretch. Then she stilled. "*News* news?"

Henri nodded.

"Right. Then let's go." Matilda was on her feet so fast the old dog let out a bark, wagged his tail, and followed as she led them away.

Andre's face wavered onto the screen and Matilda tried to work out where he was in the château, which was mentally less fraught than finding herself back in her father's office, readying herself for *more* news that would irrevocably change her life.

"Are you done with your spat?" Andre asked, settling himself in. His eyes were unusually tight, sunken, no doubt due to the middle-of-the-night hour in Chaleur.

Henri slid an arm along the back of the couch that they'd turned to face the screen on the back wall. "A mental health break is not a spat. Welcome to the twenty-first century."

As if hearing a note in Henri's voice he'd not heard before, Andre stopped fidgeting and looked at his cousin. Then at Matilda. Then at River, who was curled up on the couch beside her, forcing her to snuggle into Henri. *Good dog.*

"Let's have it," Henri growled.

Matilda shot him a glance, looking for signs of the man who'd whispered sweet nothings to her all night long, spiralling her over the edge again and again. Only to find herself looking at a prince.

"Here goes." Andre leaned back, crossed his ankle over his knee. "For a marriage to be legal in Gibraltar, you have to have been in situ for twenty-four hours."

"Which we were, right?" Matilda asked of Henri, the note of hope in her voice telling. While Henri's cheek ticked, he did not look her way, and the first shiver of concern slithered through Matilda.

"You also had to be married by a registered officiant," Andre continued. "As it turns out a ship's captain having a legal right to officiate a wedding at sea is an urban myth. In the olden days when sea journeys lasted months, it was commonplace, but no longer."

Henri's head dipped. In disappointment? Or *relief*?

Before she could check…by smacking him on the shoulder or grabbing him by the chin and saying, *Hey, remember me?* Andre said, "It turns out *our* captain, bless him, was also a licensed marriage celebrant."

Henri's head snapped back up.

"So that's it then?" Matilda asked, no longer hopeful so much as wildly anxious.

And it hit her; she wanted this, not only because of what it might mean for the future of the station, but she *wanted* it. For herself. For the life she wanted. A life with Henri.

"Not quite," said Andre, holding up a hand.

And Matilda whimpered.

Henri looked her way. *Finally.* Only his gaze was dark, hard. If he too was struggling to marry his desires and his duties, he didn't show it.

"There is also a lodging of paperwork portion to the proceedings," Andre was saying. "Which has to occur *before* your nuptials, and it was not."

Gaze locked on Henri, begging him to give

her a glimpse of the warmth beneath the facade, Matilda waited for the next twist.

She didn't have to wait long.

Andre breathed out hard, and said, "You, cousin, and Matilda, are not, and have never been, legally married."

Henri shot to his feet, leaving Matilda bereft for the lack of him beside her. She could hear her breath rushing behind her ears, could feel the blood moving under her skin. Her left hand came to her mouth as tears gathered in the corners of her eyes and panic swelled in her throat.

Her thumb began twirling the ring on her right hand the way it did when she was stressed. Henri's ring. A treasure, a talisman that had kept her connected to him across time and space. One that had never truly belonged to her.

She knew her mind ought to have gone straight to Garrison Downs, to Rose and Eve and Ana and what it meant for them that she had fallen at the first hurdle, but her gaze followed Henri as he walked around the couch, his hands on his hips, his head down, as if he too was working his way through a thousand thoughts at once.

"Cousin?" Andre said. And Matilda flinched, for she'd forgotten he was still there.

Henri looked up at the screen, his face pale. Then he closed his eyes, nodded, and said, "Thank you, Andre. Get some sleep, you look like hell.

I'll make plans to return to Chaleur as soon as possible."

What? No!

Yes, the entirety of the time they had spent together had been predicated on the marriage being valid, but this couldn't be *it*.

So much had happened, so much had changed. They'd come to know one another, truly, only for Matilda to discover that the man she'd fallen in love with was only a fraction of the man she knew now.

Yet Matilda could already feel Henri slipping away.

Andre lifted his hand in a half-hearted wave, his gaze raw, sorrowful, as if he too was disappointed in the outcome. Then the screen went black.

Matilda, her life swirling about her, plucked one thought from the air. Her mother's journal. How hard Rosamund had worked to have the life she wanted. Writing down every difficult word as if one day it might help her daughters do the same.

Matilda thought of Ana, quietly checking in. Eve quietly checking out. And Rose quietly sobbing at the thought that they might lose all of this.

But Matilda had never been quiet, and she wasn't about to start now.

"So that is that," said Henri when he finally found his voice again.

And the certainty he'd felt in Matilda's bedroom only an hour before, that whatever happened his choice would reflect his commitment to Chaleur, had turned to ice in his bones. A dark fog had closed in around the edges of his vision, as if all the colour had been leached out of his life. Readying him, no doubt, for a life of challenging service, alone, to come.

"I am sorry," he said, still unable to look at Matilda, who was vibrating on the chair he'd abandoned, "that this puts you in a difficult position. That I was not able to help you with your requirements."

"Henri," she said on a soft huff of air that coiled inside him like woodsmoke. "You have nothing to apologise for."

When she uncurled herself from the couch, he moved further away. The last thing he needed was to catch her scent, feel her warmth, as if they weren't permanently imprinted upon him. "As I told Andre, I will make my way home as soon as possible."

"That's not necessary, Henri," Matilda said, reaching for him. Whatever she saw in his face had her whipping her hand back.

"No public announcement will be required," he said, making his way through a list of things that no longer needed to take up space inside his head, as if that might ease the pressure in his chest. "This is now a private matter. My people will not be affected."

As for him? He felt as if a future world he'd been imagining had been whipped out from under him to reveal that it had been built on a false floor all along.

He clasped his hands behind his back, rolled his shoulders, and looked between her eyes. Not trusting what he might do if he looked directly into all that bright blue.

"I hereby relieve you of any bond to the crown." With that he spun on his shoe and walked away.

"Wait!"

Henri flinched but kept on walking.

"Henri, come on," she said, her voice plaintive. "Stop with the imperious prince act for just a minute and talk to me."

When every survival instinct told him to walk away and never look back, to find a way to erase all memory of her, of even the possibility of her, his one chance of having something that was truly his own, Henry slowed. Then stopped.

"Matilda, please," he said. "This needs to be clear-cut this time. I beg you."

"I know. I get it. Just…hear me out. Please."

Henri turned, breathed deeply, and looked to her.

She stood by the chair, her hands outstretched, her expression not frantic as he'd imagined. Determined. "I know we said no promises, no plans, but you have to admit that neither of us have been following *those* rules. We have been living as if this news would go the other way. Planning for it even, if only in our heads."

He breathed in, breathed out—it was the best he could do.

"Apart from the lack of a single piece of paper, nothing has really changed. I still need to help my family, and now that you are locked in to the whole prince forever deal, you need a partner. And while I know I'm not classic princess material, I'm good with people, am a quick learner, and am not afraid of hard work. I'm offering to take on that role, right now, if you'll have me."

"Matilda," he said, barely able to make words. "Do you know what you are asking?"

"Yes," she said, her voice certain. Her bright gaze holding his. "A real marriage. Not for a year, for forever."

She took a step his way, her movements careful, as if approaching a wild horse that might yet startle and bolt.

"Just think it through. Last night proved, beyond any doubt, that we are both still attracted to one another. So that side of things will not be a hardship."

Henri shifted on his feet.

"And in the years since we parted, neither of us have found anyone more compatible. Or am I speaking out of turn—"

"No," said Henri, quietly. "You are not speaking out of turn."

"I can smile and wave. I've seen enough make-over movies to know that all it takes is a little keratin and teeth-whitening strips and boom, instant princess. I also adore your country—I mean, how could I not? The thought of delving into its history, perhaps even tracing more letters like the Louis XIII, is exhilarating to me. I think I can be of value to... To the crown."

Her hand moved into his vision then, her fingers slowly sliding against his as she took him by the hand. Her right hand, then the hand wearing his mother's ring. A ring he was now certain she had worn every day since he'd gifted it to her.

"You need me, Henri. As much as I need you. We can do this. Not some fanciful summer fling, but a partnership entered into with eyes wide-open."

The terms she was offering were carefully worded, clinical—companionship, compatibility, a partnership. The complete opposite of what he had proposed, telling her all the ways he adored her while holding her tight while on the bow of a super yacht, the soft air of the Mediterranean summer fluttering her hair across her delighted eyes.

Yet he found himself actually considering it.

The joining of two esteemed families, the parameters clear. What she was suggesting was a smart choice.

A royal choice.

She squeezed his hand and he looked up.

She smiled, but there was a flicker at the corners of her eyes. Showing him what it was costing her to lay herself on the line like this. And as if seeing into the future, generations beyond, he knew that she was it for him, and always had been.

Without Matilda, he would not marry. He would not bear an heir. And Chaleur would be worse off for not having her on their side.

But by accepting this offer, he would be tying her, intentionally, to a life that was no longer her own. Unless *he* could bear the brunt. Allowing her to choose where she spent her energy. Allowing her to be herself, completely. That he *might* just be able to do.

"Promise me," he said, his words like stone over gravel, "that you will not let anyone within ten feet of you with whatever the hell keratin might be. And that you will not smile unless you damn well feel like smiling."

She blinked, then laughed. "So that's a yes?"

"Stage one would be a gentle introduction to the people of Chaleur."

Matilda swallowed, hard, but her gaze held firm.

"Stage two, a press release proclaiming our engagement. We tell the truth—we enjoyed a romantic relationship some years ago and recently reunited. Stage three, Chaleurian law requires we enter into a binding contract, the Royal Marriage

Decree, which is signed before parliament. Stage four, a royal wedding."

"And after that?" she asked, her gaze warming, then dropping to his mouth, bringing with it thoughts of the wedding night.

"And then we work hard. We live mindfully, with purpose. A life lived with a constant view to the future. Perhaps… Perhaps even an heir who, when grown, we will allow to decide for themselves, their relationship to the crown."

"A marriage," she said simply. "With plans *and* promises. I can do this. I want this."

"I want this," she'd said, not *I want you.* But he brushed it aside. Just as he had learned to brush aside his own needs, his own desires, his entire life.

Henri lifted her right hand, finding his mother's ring. When it wouldn't budge, he lifted the finger to his mouth, laved it with his tongue, then dragged the ring free with his teeth.

Two futures unfurled like ribbons before him. One in which he rose to the challenge of his position alone, and another doing so with Matilda at his side.

The decision, in the end, was no decision at all.

"Marry me, Matilda Waverly," he said, sliding the ring back onto her left hand, where it had always belonged. "Be my princess. Save your family farm."

* * *

From there it all happened fast, as fifteen thousand kilometres away in the middle of their night, the Chaleurian royal wedding machine cranked into gear.

Boris and Lars arrived at Garrison Downs within the hour, looking relieved to see both Henri *and* Matilda in one piece. Celeste—already in suit and heels as if she slept in them—was on near-permanent video call. A text to Matilda from Andre read Welcome to the family. Bonne chance!

After Henri promised Rose he would do everything in his power to make sure Matilda remained Matilda, Rose hugged Matilda harder than she'd ever hugged her before.

And thirty-six hours later, they stepped off the royal plane in Chaleur to a shimmering tarmac and pale grey skies. A light summer rain bore down upon a brass band playing a rousing song Matilda didn't know.

Standing at Henri's side, but three inches apart, as was protocol, Matilda, in a cornflower blue dress she had found in Eve's cupboard, waved as if to a crowd, rather than a line of cameras and two rows of dignitaries huddled under matching black umbrellas.

Matilda murmured, "I guess I'm not in Kansas anymore."

Henri tilted his head to hers. "There is no right

or wrong, not where you are concerned. Yes, there are traditions, and expectations, but I want us to shape this in a way that suits us. The last thing I want is for you to feel constricted."

Matilda nodded, fully aware that he was thinking of his own indoctrination into this life as a child. The way his uncle had made his life feel narrow and not his own. If *she* could help Henri not feel that way, take on some of load, it might go some way to thanking him for doing her this immense consideration. Because the balance was hugely in her favour.

Without thinking too hard about why, or whether it was the "right" thing to do, she lifted onto her toes and kissed Henri soundly on the mouth.

She felt his surprise. But then he made a sound, a soft growl that echoed inside of her, and when the stairs seemed to tip out from under her, she reached for him with her spare hand, gripping his arm.

When he pulled away his eyes were dark. Danger dark. His jaw a little tight, his smile raffish as he said, "Seems we have moved straight to Stage Two."

At the bottom of the stairs Celeste emerged as if from thin air, collecting Matilda and Boris, while Henri—with Lars at his back—was taken to meet the waiting dignitaries.

Matilda, feeling the lack of Henri like a missing limb, looped her arm through Celeste's and held on tight. "I'm so glad you're here. I'm trusting you to get me through this without tripping over some heirloom or offending the national animal of Chaleur."

"The Cerulean Chaffinch."

"Who's that?"

"Our national animal."

Of course, it was.

Andre appeared on Matilda's other side. "So, you're back. Again."

"For good this time," she said, with a smile.

"Mmm. I'd ask if you were after his money, but I know what you're worth."

Matilda laughed, a loud, not so princessy bark. "Should I be concerned he's after mine?"

Andre smiled, despite himself. "I always did like you, Matilda."

"I know you did, Andre." And it was true. Despite what he'd done, she knew his heart was in the right place. He'd been Team Henri far longer than she had.

Together they reached the town car, and Boris moved out from behind her to open her door.

Andre moved in beside Celeste as Matilda slid into the back seat. "Keep an eye on this one for me, will you?"

Celeste gripped her folder a little tighter and said nothing.

"On Matilda's side already, I see. If not for the

upcoming nuptials, I'd consider that insurrection." Andre leaned down, offering up a slow, meticulous, ever so slightly ironic bow, before he shut her door and swept away to reunite with Henri.

Celeste slid into the other side of the car and, before it had even taken off, said, "I am in charge of your schedule if you would like an update?"

"Well, I was hoping to snatch a couple of hours to work on a letter I was sent just before we left. A truly gorgeous piece purporting to have been written by Elizabeth Barret Browning—"

"Non," said Celeste.

"Non?" Matilda parroted back.

Celeste waggled a finger. "There is much to do in preparation. You require staff. An updated, or at least an expanded wardrobe. As for—" Celeste leaned in, and stage-whispered "—the wedding dress... A designer must be chosen, measurements taken. Unless..."

Celeste glanced at Matilda's belly.

"No ho-ho," said Matilda, sucking in her tummy. "Henri and I are not in preparation of that."

Not yet. Though they had spoken, in their effort at being open and communicative, about the possibility in the future.

"D'accord," said Celeste. "We also require a new passport. And a speechwriter. And—"

Matilda held up a hand to stop Celeste's diatribe. "An hour. All I need is an hour."

"I'm sure you believe that," said Celeste, her face showing emotion for the first time ever, "but life from this moment on will not be the same. For you, Matilda, are to be Princess Consort of Chaleur. A position that brings with it import, history, privilege, esteem, power. You understand this? *Oui?*"

"*Oui,*" said Matilda. For she had. At least she thought she did. She'd get there. She would.

She looked out the window to see the plane disappearing into the distance as the car swept her off the tarmac, while Henri, her touchstone in all this, was nowhere to be seen.

CHAPTER TEN

THE SUMMER FESTIVAL celebrations had begun with the summer solstice, then continued on for several weeks, with flower shows, baking contests, lake sports, fun fair rides, and the like. Upon returning from Garrison Downs, Henri agreed to take part in his fair share.

Meaning, despite his promise to himself to ease Matilda's load, he wasn't able to stop Celeste, who kept gleefully filling Matilda's calendar with meetings, lessons on the history of Chaleur, visits with stylists, and wedding planners. While anytime he saw Matilda yawn or droop, and insisted she ease back, she'd pat him on the chest, or tip onto her toes and kiss him, in an effort to distract him, before heading off to do more.

At the final event of the festival, the Annual Kinder Art Show, Henri listened with half an ear to a rather verbose patron, as a little girl with dark ringlets sidled up beside Matilda, tugged on her dress, then pointed to a painting of what looked like a tree.

Matilda's face lit up as she gathered her elegant blue velvet dress around her knees, and crouched to put herself on the girl's level.

After a short conversation, the little girl took the painting off the stand and handed it to Matilda.

Matilda's hand went to her heart. *"Pour moi?"* he heard her say. *"Merci."*

"Cinq euro," the little girl said, hand out at the end of a straight arm, chin raised, as if readying for the argument.

But Matilda had no intention of arguing. She coughed out a laugh, no doubt seeing a flicker of herself in the precocious girl. Then, glancing around, she plucked double the asking price in cash from a hidden pocket in her dress and handed it over.

The little girl's eyes widened, then she was gone, sprinting back to her parents.

Henri pressed a fist to his chest, to relieve the sudden tightness therein.

Matilda smiled at the painting, before tucking it under her arm, clearly chuffed with her purchase. She pulled herself to standing, wobbled a little on her high heels, then hid a long yawn behind the back her hand. Before she turned, breathed deep, plastered a smile on her pale face and went to find someone else to charm.

Which took half a second because the crowd enveloped her. Their impromptu kiss atop the plane stairs had hastened the timeline of their plan, and now everyone knew who Matilda Waverly was and who she would soon be.

Henri felt a moment of empathy for fairy-tale villains, for it took every ounce of royal training not to swoop in, sweep her up, take her home, lock her in their room, and force her to sleep for a week.

Andre sidled up to Henri, bowed to the patron, and carefully hustled Henri away. "Did Matilda just pay a four-year-old with cash out of her *own pocket*?"

"You must have imagined it."

"I give up."

Henri turned to his cousin. "Sorry?"

"I give up trying to protect you from yourself. I admit defeat. Your fiancée is stubborn, opinionated, uncontrollable. And now she gives from her own pocket... She's you, in a skirt."

Henri laughed, but he was so tired it came out as a sniff. "How do you think she is coping?"

"Brilliantly. Apart from the occasional rebellious flashes of ignoring protocol, or as the press are calling it, her 'rebellious Aussie flair.' She has them wrapped around her little finger. As for the rest of them—she is open, warm and they love her."

How could they not? thought Henri. And yet her capability had never been his concern.

The slow blinks. The crick of her neck. He

could see her edges beginning to fray. He might have learned to forgive himself for the rocky path he'd taken to get to this point, but he would not be able to forgive himself for that.

"She's been walking the rose garden again," he said. "In circles. Like a caged cat."

Andre clamped a hand on his shoulder. "Good for her. Now I have to nab a fine painting of a dinosaur I spotted earlier before someone swoops in and buys it out from under me."

"I'm spent." Matilda kicked off her shoes, flinging them exhaustedly across the room.

The Art Show had been fun, mostly because they'd attended it together. A rarity—since she was trying to lessen Henri's workload as much as she could, it had made sense to work separately.

When Henri didn't answer her, she looked to find him standing by the bedroom window of what had been his suite. A blend of antique and modern, neutral colours, elegance, now with her clothes draped over the back of a chair, her laptop open on the coffee table, it was slowly becoming *theirs*.

She padded across the room, and he lifted an arm, curling her into his side.

"I was just saying," she said, "it was another big day, and it's nice to see a familiar face."

"That's what I am to you?" he asked, his voice tender, his face stern.

"My demands are crazy low."

His brow furrows grew furrows. "They shouldn't be."

"Meh." Then, when she realised how truly rigid he was, she said, "Did I do something wrong?"

"You don't hum anymore."

"Hmmm?" she said, humming and yawning at once, a true time saver.

"You hum beneath your breath when you are content. And I haven't heard you hum once since we returned to Chaleur."

"Sorry," she said, yawning again. "I'll try to do better."

"No!" He turned her in his arms and looked into her face as if trying to see inside her mind. *"Stop* trying. Stop putting your hand up for so much. Stop trying to do my job for me."

"Henri, I…" Matilda lifted a hand in query, for he was being unusually contrary, and cross. "Maybe now that the Summer Festival is over things will settle."

Henri's hands ran down her velvet sleeves and back up again, goose bumps scuttling over her skin. "They won't, Matilda. This job is a merry-go-round that does not end."

"I love merry-go-rounds. Must be the horses."

It had been a lame attempt to snap him out of his funk, but the longer he stood there looking so tormented, the shakier she felt. For an engagement was not a marriage. There was time for her to screw this all up still.

She breathed out hard. "I thought I was kind of nailing the pre-princess thing."

"You are," he said, his gaze wretched and beautiful and tragic and hot. "You are. *You* are perfect."

At which point he growled and gathered her in his arms, lifting her and carrying her to his bed. *Their bed.* He dropped her there with a soft bounce. On the cloud-soft mattress and baby seal eyelash blanket—or whatever unbelievably lush fibre it was made from.

Then he stood at the end of the bed, his hair a little mussed, his tie skew-whiff.

She tilted her head at his shirt. "You have a button undone." Because she'd undone it, when canoodling at the window.

And after a few fraught seconds, in which Matilda thought she might faint from desire, he undid the rest. Slowly.

By the time he peeled the shirt away, revealing sculpted shoulders and flat pecs covered in a smattering of dark hair, the kind that trailed away to a point below the button of his suit pants, she was at the edge of the bed on her knees.

"Pants," she said, fingers clicking, gaze glued to the need pressing against his zip.

He snapped the top button, yanked down his zip, then paused. The way his favoured black

Y-fronts framed him, just so, deserved awards. All of them.

She looked up. "If you are waiting for me to say *Your Highness*, you've got a long wait coming."

Henri smiled, the furrows softening.

And Matilda was sure, despite any hiccups and speed bumps and the haste with which they had been forced to figure this all out, *this* part they had down pat. Meaning surely the rest would follow.

Then, as if he couldn't wait, he came to her, drawing her higher on her knees so he could slide his hands into her hair and tilt her face to his so that he could kiss her. Lush, deep, narcotic kisses that went on for days.

Then he pressed her back as he climbed over her, onto the bed. Settling himself over her. Kissing her eyelids, her cheeks, her nose, as if making sure she was all there.

Please work out, she thought, with a soul deep ache that she understood all too well. *Please, please, please*.

For she loved this man. A love that was wild and gentle, consuming and thoughtful, eternal and new. All at once.

She'd loved him as long as she could remember and, if he'd let her, would keep on doing so for the rest of her life.

Then she gathered him to her and rolled so that he lay back on the bed, the Superman curl falling over one eye.

"I wasn't so sure about this dress," she said, straddling him and wriggling in a way that had him sucking in breath, the pale hazel of his eyes turning to pure smoke. "Till I realised it meant I could do this."

Reaching beneath one knee, then the other, she whipped off her underpants, twirled them over her head, and flung them to the other side of the room.

Then, sliding her hands over his hips, she shimmied his suit pants down just enough to set him free. Tracing the smooth length slowly, reverently, before she gathered up the layers of her blue velvet skirt and lifted to notch herself against him.

He took her hips in his hands, his nostrils flaring, his gaze adoring as she sank down, slowly, inch by inch, taking him, all of him. Till she felt full, rippling with beautiful certainty, that she was exactly where she was meant to be.

Henri sat up, and she gasped as he went deeper still.

Clutching him to her, she rocked, biting her lip to stop from crying out. So soon. Too soon.

He reached behind her, gathering her hair over one shoulder and sliding the zip from neck to the top of her buttocks. His fingers tracing her spine. And as he rolled the fabric down her arms, taking one breast into his warm mouth, then the other, the sounds he made, raw and primal, turned her to pure liquid.

The late evening sunshine poured into his room through the large windows creating a golden haven, as if even the season was blessing them.

And they made love. Delicate touches, eyes open, breaths shared. A slow, sensuous coming together that made Matilda feel as if her DNA had dissolved and been put back together differently.

When pleasure pooled inside of her, it was like a dark lagoon, bottomless and ancient. But she held on, feeling him build, and when she thought he might break, she pressed a hand to his hip and rocked back, and together they breached time and space, as she'd always known they would.

Later that night, after a long, leisurely joint shower, they curled into one another beneath the soft sheets. And Matilda saw a familiar book on Henri's bedside table. Blue leather. The collection of letters and poems she had bought him all those years ago. The one he'd claimed to have lost.

Only it seemed it had been found, after all.

Matilda tried to catch Henri's eye through the crowd of people who had crammed into the Royal Room of Parliament House, most speaking in Chaleurian-accented French so she could only pick up a phrase here and there.

Not that she minded, as it let her switch off for a few blessed moments.

Henri had been right about life not letting up

after the festival, it had only become more frenetic. If this was the pace that she'd be expected to set, then she'd simply needed to make some changes. Exercise. Eat better. And sleep a whole lot more. Or the first two at least. For the nights in Henri's bed—their bed—made every hidden yawn worth it.

"Ms. Waverly." The Minister of State's hand hovered near an intricately carved chair. "Sit here, please."

Matilda took the proffered seat in front of the magnificent desk, one that gave her father's a run for its money. The room, in which every royal decree for the past two hundred years had been signed, was gilt-edged at every chance, the walls decked in marble columns, and the amount of red velvet hanging from the windows was almost suffocating.

Then there was the large piece of paper sitting benignly in front of her. A3, off-white, with a faint raised watermark and House of Raphael-Rossetti royal seal, and a short paragraph declaring her intention to wed Henri, and his to wed her, with spaces prepared for two signatures and a witness.

According to Celeste, once the contract was signed, their marriage was set in stone. The royal wedding, which had been in the planning since the day they'd left Garrison Downs, was for the people. This was for the law.

Matilda shook out her hands to get some blood to her fingers. Not that she was nervous. She was ready. For once the contract was signed, her part in satisfying the condition of bequeathment of her father's will was done.

After that, the rest of her life would be about her and Henri. Henri, who for all his attentiveness, his patience, had been slowly reverting back to the Henri he'd been when she'd met him on the street in Côte de Lapis.

Maybe it was nerves. Maybe he was having second thoughts. Maybe this was all a dream. She surreptitiously pinched herself on the wrist.

And reminded herself that she was here. That this was real.

And that she loved him. Had done before she'd known he was a prince. Before she'd even known his real name. And every day she spent with him, watching him work, learning his mind, holding him through the night, she loved him more.

Maybe she ought to have told him by now. So that he knew she wasn't doing this *only* to help her sisters. Told him that asking him to marry her was the single best choice she had ever made.

But the thing was, while she knew that he liked her, respected her, was attracted to her, and that he needed her, beyond that she wasn't *entirely* sure of the exact shape of his feelings for her.

But that was something she would think about tomorrow. Or after the wedding. Or when interest in their relationship cooled and they were both able to come up for air.

Matilda tugged at the neckline of her dress, where it had begun to itch. Chaleurian red, dainty lace, a high neck, fitted bodice and layers of tulle. A little fancy for her taste but it was a moment of historical import and she did not want to give Henri a moment's pause.

Henri, who was still nowhere to be seen.

Her heart was beating a little fast for comfort now. And she could feel sweat pooling in unmentionable places. If only she could see Henri, take a minute, maybe slip away into a room nearby to talk. To hold his hands and look him in the eye, feel the connection she felt sure of when it was just the two of them. Then maybe she *could* tell how she felt, before they signed this paper. Make a private promise to be his forevermore—

A bell rang, and Matilda flinched.

It was a light golden tinkle compared with the hearty rumble of the Homestead bell of Garrison Downs. Though this crowd understood its meaning, everyone quieting and finding their place around the edges of the room.

And then there he was. *Henri.*

No. In his midnight blue three-piece suit, his matinee hair perfect, his cut-glass jaw tight and unsmiling, he was most certainly Prince Henri Gaultier Raphael-Rossetti, the Sovereign Prince of Chaleur.

She caught his eye and tried for a smile herself, but her mouth wobbled, as nerves now well and truly had her in their clutch.

His brow creased as he noted the trembling of her hands, and she quickly dropped them to her lap.

When he took the seat beside hers, a camera flash went off and Matilda blinked. Then the Minister of State began speaking in French, then again in English, but by then her heart was beating so hard his words were all muffled.

Matilda glanced at Henri to find him staring at the paper in front of them, his skin pale, none of that flush of lovely pink in his cheeks that she loved so much. Now even his brow furrows were smoothed away, as if he was running on backup power.

She opened her mouth to check if he was okay, when the bell rang again.

And the Minister called her name.

"Matilda Lavigne Waverly, do you consent to enter the state of matrimony with Prince Henri Gaultier Raphael-Rossetti, and in doing so agree to become a citizen of Chaleur and to dedicate your life to its people? If so, sign your name to the Royal Marriage Decree."

Matilda glanced back at Henri, to find him still staring ahead. The people watching, the stuffiness of the room began to make her feel as if the room was tipping. She reached for the pen, clicked the nib into place, and—

"Wait." Henri's voice cut though the quiet like a scythe.

Matilda's pen hovered over the contract as a collective gasp echoed through the room. "Henri, are you...?" Matilda swallowed. "Are you talking to me?"

His chin dropped, his hands clenching and un-clenching on the table. And fear flashed inside her like a warning flare on a clear night at sea.

Then Henri declared, "Can we please have the room?"

And it was done within seconds. A hush of shuffling feet and muted whispers, then the snick of the door. And they were alone. Just as she'd wished only a moment before.

The marble and velvet and glints of gold made the room feel hot and cold all at once. Or maybe that was just her. Adrenaline and mortification a throbbing cocktail inside of her.

"Henri?"

Henri turned to her, *finally*, his expression now ravaged with emotion. "I should never have let it get this far."

Oh, God. Oh, no. "What? What do you mean?"

He who was so afraid of pitting a single foot wrong, he had worked himself to the bone. What he had just done would reverberate through the halls of this place in a nanosecond.

Henri reached for her then, but she snapped her arm away, the pen clattering to the desk. Then she pushed her chair back, hard enough that it rocked before settling on an angle.

And she began to pace. Hands on hips, dragging in breath—not an easy feat considering the snug fit of the damned red lace dress. Tendrils dangled damply from her updo. Her knees hurt as her shoes were that smidge too high.

When Henri stood, all elegance and grace, he did not reach for her again.

"Matilda, I've had decades to prepare for this role, to truly understand the sacrifice. No matter how much I've fought it, I *was* born for this. And it's so clear to me now that forcing this life on you was the most selfish thing I have ever done. I cannot watch you walk barefoot circles in the rose garden, like a caged cat. I just can't."

The rose garden?

What was he talking about?

Matilda smacked a hand to her chest. "I made this decision. I'm the one who practically *begged* you to marry me. If you didn't see the value in what I can offer, or couldn't imagine how we can make this work, long term, you might have said so before I came back here with you. Before I sat there."

Henri's jaw worked. "I will give you access to the best lawyers—"

"Don't. Do not. If you are really doing what

I think you're doing, then I want nothing from you."

"But your situation—"

"I can count on both hands the number of nice local men, whose land isn't nearly as profitable as ours, who would jump at the chance of marrying into the Waverly family money."

Henri's cool evaporated from one blink to the next. His voice was dangerously low as he said, "Is that what you want?"

"Of course not!" She was merely trying to unhinge him as he'd unhinged her. "Henri, look at me. Look at where I am right now. If you can't see what I want, and the lengths I've been willing to go to get it…"

She wanted the whirlwind, and the settling afterward. The ache and the joy she'd read about in love letters. She wanted a partner who chose her the way she chose him. She wanted all that, with Henri.

"You forget," said Henri, his jaw taking on a stubborn set, "that I have now seen you on horseback, traipsing about in your gum boots, sassing your sister, snuggled up on the back porch with your lovely old dog. There you have space and air and time to do the work that inspires you."

Matilda swallowed back the tears that were threatening to spill, for she had to get through this. "And if I don't want that? What if I told you that I love exhausting myself and having to think on the fly and living by deadlines. Why are you the only one for whom that is allowed?"

"Because I have lived it, pushed it away, taken it back, and chosen it. As it has chosen me. But you..."

He held her gaze, his expression so intense he might as well have been holding her. For she could feel him with every part of her. "You can do anything, Matilda. Anywhere. Your life can be as vast as you want it to be. But not if you are here. Not with me."

Matilda opened her mouth to argue, but then it hit her.

It took two to make a marriage work. Two people who woke up every day and, despite the challenges life threw at them, said, *Yes. This. Together.* And Henri did not look in any place to be saying *yes.* In fact, he looked determined to go into battle. Against her.

She loved him. She would marry him in a heartbeat. On a yacht. In this ridiculously opulent room. In the ballroom back home. Up a tree. Down a well.

But he was trying to make it clear to her that he would not marry her.

And it didn't matter how he felt about her, or maybe it was because of how he felt about her, he had it in his head that it would be best for her if he let her go.

And she knew, in that moment, she could push

him, she could twist him, she could convince him he was wrong. But unless he came to that conclusion on his own, he'd hate himself for it for the rest of his life.

She would sacrifice herself for her sisters, but she would not sacrifice him.

Heart beating in her throat, skin clammy, tears now streaming unimpeded down her face, Matilda asked, "Are you certain this is what you want?"

The look in his eyes—those beautiful soulful poetic eyes—told her all she needed to know.

So, Matilda did what Matilda did when faced with desperate situations—she hitched up her dress and fled.

CHAPTER ELEVEN

HENRI GRIPPED THE ancient stone rampart of the highest keep of Château de Chaleur, looking south over the dark, moon-kissed forest below.

After Matilda had fled the Royal Room of Parliament House, he'd had to stay back, asking for everyone's patience and assuring them that the country could go on in the knowledge that their prince was neither fickle nor a fool.

Now he had to convince himself. For while he knew that letting her go, giving her the chance to choose a different life, an easier life, a freer life, was the right thing to do, why did it feel so damnably wrong?

Andre's whistle heralded his arrival.

"Is she gone?" Henri asked.

"Boris drove her away an hour ago."

Henri's head dropped, his shoulders hunched, his fingers gripping hard enough to scrape.

"Want to talk about it?" Andre asked.

"So that you might smugly say *I told you so*?"

Andre reared back. "Do you think this is an outcome I approve of?"

Henri folded his arms as he turned to face his cousin, preferring to send all the ire that he felt with himself in that direction for a spell.

"Do you not remember me telling you that after you first set eyes on Matilda Waverly, right after scraping your molten heart off the floor, that I would make it my mission to find out who she was, where she came from, her net worth, and the...the name of the doctor who'd set her broken arm when she was seven."

"She broke her arm when she was seven?" How had he not known that? No, he couldn't start thinking about all the things they'd yet to learn about one another, or he'd go mad from missing her. And she'd only been gone an hour.

"My point, cousin, is—did you not wonder why it took me so long to find out that Henri Gaultier and Matilda Waverly did not have a Gibraltarian marriage license?"

Henri looked to Andre. Then looked harder. "Are you saying—"

"The moment you brought her through the château doors, it was clear that you still had feelings for her. While I stand by what I did all those years ago, it's sat inside me like a stone every day since... Matilda is good for you. She brings levity and balance and looks at you like you hang the blooming stars and moon. I considered giving you the time you needed to come to that conclusion on your own as my atonement."

When Henri had no comeback, Andre went on. "Which for you, dear cousin, took ten times longer than it ought, for you are a stubborn bastard with a martyr complex."

Andre droned on about Augustus "doing a number" on him and "classic transference," saying things Henri knew to be true, only didn't have the emotional vocabulary to verbalise.

Or *hadn't* for a long time. For he'd locked his feelings away in a place so deep he'd not recognised them when they had reemerged.

Feelings. Such an anaemic way to say that he loved her.

Because Henri loved Matilda. And had always loved her.

It was that complex and that simple, all at once.

Henri blanched. "I've let that voice in the back of my head, the one telling me that I am not allowed to enjoy being a prince, to make my decisions for me. Haven't I?"

Aw, hell.

"A *martyr* complex, you say?"

"Boom!" Andre held out both hands in revelation. "Just call me your fairy godfather."

"I'd rather not."

"Are you sure? Because I feel as if I have finally hit my straps—"

"I am sure. Now I need you to stop talking so I can figure out how the hell I can fix this."

"The plan, before you blew it up spectacularly, was to marry Matilda, make babies, live happily ever after. Why does that have to change?"

So much for not playing fairy godfather. And yet…the man was damnably good at it.

Henri strode to the stairs and hastened his pace as he made his way down, the cold of the ancient stone matching the cold in his limbs. The fear that he'd gone too far. That no matter what he might say to her, to explain himself, she'd finally hit her limit.

When he reached his suite—their suite—he found signs of the lack of her: the space where her laptop had charged, her messed-up side of the bed, the red lace dress she'd been wearing now draped over the back of a chair.

He'd told Matilda what he was feeling, but only to a point. For he'd not given her all the pertinent information. She deserved to know *why* he was so desperate for her to live the life she wanted.

Because he loved her. Deeply, desperately.

His job was not to fix things for her so that they were perfect. It was to trust her to make her own choices. And if they included him, he would wrap her up tight and love her so hard and be grateful every damn day.

He patted his pocket, looking for his phone to call Boris, to find out where they were, but having come directly from Parliament his phone was likely still in Celeste's care.

Dammit.

He searched for another way. Another means to get through to her…there. Beside the landline phone on his side of the bed sat a small, blue book, filled with letter and poems.

He grabbed the book, the tome fitting in his hand like it was made for that purpose, then crossed the room to sit at his desk. Where he pulled out a piece of paper, his personal stationery.

And he sat down and started to write.

It had taken a depressingly short time for Matilda to pack her bag. As if she'd been quietly concerned she'd not be there that long.

Only this time, rather than fleeing home and hiding within the safe cocoon of her family, she'd asked Boris to find her a hotel. Someplace close that she could hole up and think.

Because, despite her earlier certainty that giving Henri what he wanted was the most honourable thing that she could do, every minute that passed she felt more certain that what he *thought* he wanted was just plain wrong.

No questions asked, Boris had put her up in an apartment in Côte de Lapis owned by "the family," for it was secure, and the staff had been vetted and would know to keep her presence there private.

Matilda dumped her bags and trudged to the window seat, the Mediterranean dark, lights from the cafés and cars below creating a golden glow. And there she sat, curled up, licking her wounds. And trying to figure out where she'd gone so wrong.

The urge to call her sisters was there, as it likely always would be. Eve would tell it like it was. Ana would be sweet as hell. Rose would open her arms. But that's not what she needed. For this was on her.

She looked down at the ring she'd not thought to give back as she'd fled the Royal Room. The one Henri had given her several years ago. Had watched her toying with over the past weeks and never asked her to return.

Henri would never have done what he did lightly. Or without reason, deeply felt. Especially not to her. She'd seen the trauma in his eyes as he'd cut her free.

But he was also hyperaware of his place in history. And determined to never put himself ahead of the needs of others the way his forebears had. *To a fault.*

She sat forward, hugging her knees as puzzle pieces began to shift and move before settling into a new shape.

Was it possible that she made him *happy*, and he just didn't know what to do with it?

She coughed out a half sob, half laugh. For

with a little distance and a little air, a little time away from his consuming presence, it *all* made such perfect sense.

Henri collated work with duty. Happiness with frivolity. And family with pain.

Marrying her, making her a part of his family, must have messed with his head, big-time. Especially since he cared for her. And, as he'd attested, wanted her to the live the best life she possibly could.

It had never occurred to him that her best life was with him.

Matilda uncurled herself from the window seat, her feet tingling with pins and needles as she tapped her toes to the floor, her legs jiggling as she tried to think her way through what it meant.

If only, rather than retreating, protecting *herself*, she'd been brave enough to tell him how she felt. That she loved him with every last bit of her soul. That she wanted to be with him wherever that might be. And that deep down, she had been sure enough of his feelings for her that she'd bet the station on it. Then she might be finally, legally, hitched to the guy by now.

Only now it was too late. Or was it? Weren't second chances, and third chances, part of the deal, if you loved someone enough?

There was only one way to find out. She switched on her phone screen, readying to call Andre, or Celeste, or Boris—

When a knock came to her door.

It was the porter, holding out a small package, wrapped in brown paper with a string tie.

"Are you sure this is for me?"

The porter nodded. *"Oui, mademoiselle."*

Only Boris knew where she was, meaning it had to be from him. Or someone he worked for.

Her knees a little wobbly, Matilda hurried back to the window seat, sat cross-legged, and opened the package to find a familiar, small, beaten-up, blue book of poetry.

Pulse fluttering in her wrists, behind her knees, in her belly, she opened the book and a piece of paper fell out.

A letter.

Written on stationery from the desk of Prince Henri Gaultier Raphael-Rossetti of the Royal House of Chaleur in Henri's own hand.

Matilda,

I offer you these words, even while knowing that you of all people, have read so many efforts at saying what I wish to say, from the pens of far better writers than I. And yet that will not stop me, for I trust that you will feel the truth in them. And at this point, after the mistakes that I have made, my truth is all I have left to offer you.

I asked you to wait, as I wanted you to be sure. Not stubbornly sacrificing your life for the sake of your sisters, or generously stepping into a role that you knew would serve me. Sure, for you.

Sure, the way I am, and have been, for as long as I can remember, that being together is the thing you want most in the world.

Despite my struggles with the concept of fate—after being told my entire life that I was "meant to be" a prince—I walked into a club in Vienna and saw the woman I knew would change my life. Right in the moment I was ready for change.

Then, a few short weeks ago, while driving in Le Côte de Lapis, as I once again found myself in a moment of fractured time, of deep uncertainty, there you were again. A glance, a smile, a nod building the foundations beneath me that I had been missing.

How could I, a man unmanned by you, have hoped to offer a woman such as you the same foundations, the same certainty, the same protection and promises of forever? All of which you deserved.

Now, as I imagine you slipping further and further from my reach, all I can do is offer you what you have given me—care, faith, understanding, and as many chances as you need to be sure. Sure that a life with me, and all that that brings with it, including my heart and soul, is enough.

On my knees, I offer you my life, and the chance to share yours.
A life full of promises and plans.
Yours. In entirety. For eternity.
Henri

Matilda closed the piece of paper, folding it along the crease lines, carefully, before she brought it and the book to her chest. Holding it close as tears poured down her face.

This, from a man taught to be careful with his words. To behave and be proper and keep himself apart. Her pragmatic prince with the heart of a poet had finally, finally, stepped out of his head and into her heart.

And just like that, all the feelings she'd been holding inside released, hot and wild, like the blast of an explosion.

She'd loved Henri since the moment she'd set eyes on him. And feelings like that didn't just go away. They subsided like a flame starved of oxygen, and they waited. Waited until they were once again given air. Sunshine by a seaside town. A library filled with the dust and whispers of history. Boat rides on a crystalline lake. Tenderness, conversation, care.

And now they burned inside of her like a storm.

She uncurled herself from the window seat once more and spun in a circle. Looking for... what? Her phone. To call him?

Or call Boris to come and get her, so that she might storm the castle, literally.

Oh, did she want to call Rose—tell her everything truly *was* going to work out! Or Eve, to tell her to get the heck over herself, call Ana to tell her to make friends, go home, and stop being so isolated, because being brave and opening yourself up gave you the best chance at being happy.

Because she wanted them all to feel this good. Only it was not her job to pull the wheels and levers to make that happen. Not anymore.

It was her job to do whatever it took to make sure *she* was happy. And the good would flow from there.

Stage One—go get her man.

Henri paced the foyer of the château.

"Anything?" he barked, when Celeste dared to pop her head out into the hall.

She shook her head. Then shushed someone behind her before saying, "Though your cousin wishes for me to tell you that it is late, and you have a big day tomorrow what with that meeting with the Minister for Agriculture and the board of governors of the children's hospital we visited a few weeks ago and—"

"Tell your ventriloquist dummy to grab his keys, he's driving."

For since leaving to drop the book to Matilda, after refusing to give up where she was—the man's loyalties were seriously skewed, and yet, such that Henri wanted to give him a medal— Boris was not answering his phone. And Henri did not trust himself behind the wheel.

"Where exactly is he meant to be driving you? Your cousin wonders."

Anywhere. Everywhere. Till he found her and told her, in person, what he'd said in that damnable letter. Had it been a mistake? Too cryptic? Would she think it cowardly? Or would she understand that he wanted to connect with her in the ways that had meaning for her?

Then...

Was that a car door?

A few moments later Boris came through the door and, with a bow and a slight smile, said, "A delivery for you, Your Highness."

He stepped aside, and...

"Matilda."

In place of the red lace dress, she wore jeans and a T-shirt, flat shoes, her hair down, her face scrubbed of makeup. The kind of clean that came not only from soap and water, but from tears.

His heart ached at the knowledge he'd done that, his decision-making so poor.

After saying something to Boris that made him blush, Matilda's gaze lifted and found Henri's and everything else melted away.

He took a step, then another, then she ran to him, and she threw herself into his arms. Kissing his cheeks, his jaw, his mouth. Peppering him as if it might be her last chance.

The momentum rocked him back, before he gathered himself, and her, twirling her around and around and around.

When they slowed, the world slowed with them. Slowed, then settled. Like a tornado in reverse. The pieces sifting into perfect place.

Her tiptoes touched the ground, then with her arms still around his neck, she pulled back just enough to look into his eyes.

Henri didn't need to ask for the room, not this time. He could sense those who knew him best, his chosen family, who supported and care for him—not the crown, him—made themselves scarce.

"I'm so glad you didn't leave," he said.

"I'm so glad you wrote to me." She lifted one hand from his neck to show that she held the book, worn blue leather, the corner of his letter poking out the top.

He grimaced. "I'm more of a political writer—speeches, arguments and the like. Letters have never been my forte."

"Oh," she said, pressing herself against him, her eyes heavy, her teeth hooking against her lower lip, "I can assure you they are. And I'm an expert, you know."

"So I've heard." Henri drank her in. His Matilda, here, in his arms. Where—now that he'd seen the alternative—it was so clear that she was meant to be. "I meant every word I wrote."

"I know," she said, her fingers playing with his hair.

"Despite how it might have seemed in the Room of Royal Decree, there is nothing I want more than to have you in my life, Matilda."

"I know," she said again, this time her voice had a little burr.

"Not least of all, is because I am in love with you. And have been for a good portion of my life."

A dreamy smile flashed over her face before she said, "I know that too."

"You know a lot, as it turns out," he said, sliding a hand down her back.

"I do, in fact," she said, her voice getting that languorous edge that he loved so much. "Whereas you have some catching up to do. Such as that thing you said, about me walking barefoot circles in the rose garden—I do that not because I feel trapped, but because it reminds me so much of my mum's rose garden back home. That's all. I'm happy here, Henri. I want this. I want you."

Henri breathed out, relief flooding through him. That she knew him. Understood him. Had come back to him.

"And it would pay to remember that," she said, "so that next time you feel the urge to self-sacrifice for no good reason, you can look to me and I'll knock the thought right out of your head. In a loving way."

Henri's heart lurched in his chest. "In a loving way, you say."

Matilda nodded beatifically. Then a slow smile eased its way across her lovely face. "I love you, Henri. I loved you when you were a young man so desperate to find your direction. I loved you still when I saw how big your fairy-tale castle was."

He pulled her in a little tighter. "Is that so?"

"Mmm hmm. When I knew that it was inevitable, that the feelings you bring out in me, the way you conduct yourself, the man that you are had ruined me for all other men, was when we were ambling to the stables back home. You in what you thought was Outback chic, dust motes swishing past that face of yours in the hazy afternoon light, and then you accepted poor Beryl as your mount, without complaint...that was it for me, Henri. I was done."

Henri leaned down and pressed a featherlight kiss against her lips. Because he wanted to, and because he could. Then he lifted his hand to cup her face and kissed her properly.

The true sealing of their promise.

"That's it then," he murmured against her lips. "If I love you, and you love me, then we definitely make it official. Don't you think?"

She blinked up at him. "I've thought so for

some time. But...do we have to sign that thing in that room?"

Henri understood her hesitation and was determined to do whatever it took to do it their way. "I believe we do but—"

"No," said Celeste popping her head out from the sitting room once more. For it seems they had not made themselves as scarce as he'd assumed.

"No?" said Matilda, peering around Henri's side.

"You do not."

Andre came out from behind Celeste, his hand sliding from around her waist. That was new. Or perhaps not, now that he thought about it.

"It is tradition, yes," said Andre, "but there is no law that says you must. Hey, Matilda."

"Hey, Andre. You been hiding in there the whole time?"

"Yes, I have."

"Then be of use, will you," said Henri.

And the way Matilda grinned, as if her heart bloomed at the sight of him being impertinent made him certain this was going to be a hell of a ride.

"Whatever Matilda wants, make it happen."

"We would like to sign the contract here," Matilda added, "an intimate affair, with witnesses of our choosing."

"*D'accord,*" said Celeste, wincing a little at the move away from protocol as she took notes.

"Did she just curtsy?" Matilda whispered.

"I think she did."

"The wedding can still be a total blowout though."

Celeste looked up, her expression hovering close to true joy.

"I am so happy to hear that," she said, her fingers tapping madly over her phone.

"Only can we bring the timeline up?" Matilda added, her hand moving into the back of his hair. "As soon as humanly possible. Gotta lock this one down."

At that, Celeste grinned. "We can do anything."

"I like the sound of that," said Matilda, before leaning her ear against his chest and holding him.

Henri liked the sound of it too.

EPILOGUE

Chaleur,
late August

THE LEAD-IN to their wedding day was a beautiful blur.

When Henri explained to parliament that his hesitancy over signing the contract in such a formal space had been due to his intention to curate his sovereignty with a more contemporary bent, they had kindly taken him at his word.

The day itself boasted enough pomp to include crowns, sceptres, blessings from religious leaders and government officials, lots of papers to sign and promises made regards standing for the people of Chaleur.

Yet it was also heart-warmingly intimate.

With Chaleur being a country of artisans, Matilda could happily have chosen dresses by a dozen local designers, but in the end went with a floaty cream number Celeste had found her, with elbow-length sleeves and a cinched waist, the skirt falling in soft layers.

Henri had Andre as his best man. While, despite it being on the verge of spring on the station,
and her sister working so hard to cement her position as the boss of Garrison Downs, Rose had
moved heaven and earth to be there. To stand up
beside Matilda as her witness, her maid of honour.

Eve, it turned out, *had* booked a flight home,
back to Garrison Downs, for the first time in far
too long, so couldn't be there, but in a rare and
much appreciated message had sent her congratu-
lations and promised Matilda she would "gorge"
herself on what was sure to be an obscene number of photos as soon as she landed.

Since none of them wanted to swing any undue
attention Ana's way, she stayed home. Though
Matilda—already good to go on the ring side of
things—had asked Ana if she could make Henri's
wedding ring. Which she'd been tearily delighted
to do.

Matilda did not have anyone give her away.
She wanted it to be clear that this choice was
very much her own.

They'd made their way, in horse and carriage
no less, to the Cathédrale de Chaleur, in which
the wedding was to take place. Then, once the
dresser and hair and makeup people had finally
swept out of the anteroom, leaving Matilda and
Rose alone for the first time all day, the sisters
looked at one another across the small room.

With tears in her eyes, Rose began to laugh as she took in the frescoes and antiques everywhere they looked. "Does this even feel real to you?"

"One gets used to it."

Rose's gaze dropped back to Matilda. "Does one?"

Matilda poked out her tongue.

"Well." Rose moved in and took Matilda by both hands, eyes roving over her beautiful boho dress, the Australian wildflowers in her hair. "You look so disgustingly happy I can't stand it."

"I am," Matilda said, squeezing Rose's hand only to find it cool and shaky, unlike her own. "Deeply, truly, revoltingly happy."

Matilda turned to look at herself in the mirror. Then she beckoned Rose to stand beside her; the colour of Rose's simple, sleek copper dress so reminiscent of the way Garrison Downs land looked when the sun hit just so, it was as if her sisters, her mum, and her dad, were a part of the day too.

"I will miss making life brighter, and easier for you all," said Matilda.

Rose snorted. "You, darling sister, were never easy."

Matilda grinned. "Yeah, you're probably right."

"If Mum and Dad could see you now, they would be so damn proud. Not that you've landed a prince, though Mum would have *loved* that. They'd be so chuffed that you figured out what you want, then went out and got it. That is the Waverly way."

Matilda reached back for Rose's hand and Rose rested her chin on Matilda's shoulder. "Despite their rocky road, they really did eat life up with a spoon, didn't they. A good example for us all."

And then it was time.

The grand organ stuck a familiar tone, Celeste swept into the room, made sure they had their bouquets—a mix of delicate native Chaleurian wildflowers, ivy from the stone walls outside the château, and imported Sturt's desert peas, fields of which could be found all around Garrison Downs—and hustled Rose, then Matilda, into place.

Henri, with Andre at his side, looked impossibly dashing. All broad shoulders, and brow furrows; so utterly Byronic it was a miracle her knees didn't give out from under her.

The hot hard gaze of his eyes making her certain that, like her, he could not wait for the official bit to be over so that they might truly start their lives together.

As husband and wife. Prince and princess. Henri and Tilly. Mad for each other and happy for the world to see it.

The ceremony itself went on as such ceremonies tended to do.

The moment Henri reoffered Matilda his mother's ring, this time it came with the knowledge of all of the history and the love and the burden that it entailed, which made it all the more special.

When she placed the ring Ana had made onto Henri's finger, she felt her fractured family click into place. As if rising from the ashes of the horrors of the past few months, it had been made anew.

They left the cathedral under a confetti of dried peony petals, before making it down the steps and out onto the beachside strip of le Côte de Lapis, where thousands of Chaleurians clapped and cheered. With Boris and Lars hovering not too far behind, Henri and Matilda shook hands, accepted flowers and wishes of *bonne chance* from people it was now her official duty to care for.

"They do love you," Matilda told Henri as she took him by the arm.

"It's you they love," he insisted, pressing a quick kiss to her hair. "Listen."

Voices called. *"Princess! Princess Matilda, over here! Je t'adore!"*

But while Matilda was honestly delighted, she was also only half listening, her focus on her husband and the expression on his face. How at ease he finally was.

She lifted to press a kiss to his cheek, then tucked herself into his side, which drew a huge cheer from the crowd.

True love, it turned out, wasn't all whirlwinds,

and fluttering hearts, and high adventure. It was opening herself to someone, letting them see to the heart of her, and working hard to see to the heart of them. Flaws and all.

Then choosing that person again and again.

Every single day.

Every moment.

For ever after.

Which she knew she'd have no problem doing at all.

* * * * *

*Look out for the next story
in the One Year to Wed quartet*
Reluctant Bride's Baby Bombshell
by Rachael Stewart

*And if you enjoyed this story,
check out these other great reads
from Ally Blake*

Cinderella Assistant to Boss's Bride
Fake Engagement with the Billionaire
Whirlwind Fling to Baby Bombshell

All available now!